Full Circle

Full Circle

Gila Diamond

FELDHEIM PUBLISHERS Jerusalem / New York

Library of Congress Cataloging-in-Publication Data

Diamond, Gila.
Full circle / by Gila Diamond.
p. cm.
ISBN 0-87306-690-1. — ISBN 0-87306-691-X (pb)
1. Children of Holocaust survivors—United States—Fiction.
2. Married women—United States—Fiction. 3. Jewish women—United States—Fiction. 4. Infertility—Fiction. I. Title.
PS3554.I235F85 1994
813'.54—dc20 94-22920

First published 1994

FELDHEIM PUBLISHERS
POB 35002 / Jerusalem, Israel

200 Airport Executive Park
Nanuet, NY 10954

Typesetting/Layout: Astronel, Jerusalem

Printed in Israel

10 9 8 7 6 5 4 3 2 1

This book is dedicated
to the memory of my mother ע"ה.
May her merits be an advocate
for me, her daughter,
and for all of her descendants.

Although written as a novel, this story is true. Names and various details have been changed to insure the privacy of the individuals involved. "Gila Diamond" is the author's pseudonym.

ACKNOWLEDGMENTS

THE ONE MAJOR drawback to having written this book under a pseudonym is that I cannot thank by name those who have contributed so much to the actualization of this book. However, those nearest and dearest to me will surely know that I am the author and I would like to acknowledge them as best I can.

My parents have led lives that were fraught with difficulties and challenges. They utilized these challenges to grow and become ever closer to Hashem. They were the paragons of *middas ha-gevurah*, and whatever I have been able to internalize from their example in this regard has served me well through my own years of challenge.

My husband built on my parents' foundation. With his *middas ha-chesed* he always reached out to help others overcome their suffering and therefore he himself never became depressed during our years of childlessness. His way of handling our mutual pain prevented me from slipping into total despair. May Hashem grant him the strength to continue to inspire others to serve Hashem *be-simchah*.

My close friends remained loyal to me at a time when I needed to take more than I was able to give. They also did not allow my self-image to become distorted as a result of my pain. They remained true to who they were and helped me to maintain my self-respect. I would especially like to thank the friend who not only taught me everything I know about word processing, but who has also taught me what it means to have true generosity of spirit.

My special thanks to Mr. Yaakov Feldheim, his editor-in-chief Marsi Tabak, copyeditor Joyce Bennett, art director Harvey Klineman, and all the staff members at Feldheim Publishers for their superb editing, design and production of my book.

Where have all the flowers gone
Long time passing
Where have all the flowers gone
Long time ago

Where have all the flowers gone
Young girls have picked them every one
When will they ever learn
Oh, when will they ever learn

The time was the sixties. This was its song. I was just a young girl when I first heard it sung. I was sitting in the school bus and a girl, a few years older than me, was sitting nearby, hunched over her guitar. She sang this song beautifully and with great emotion.

In my childish innocence, I thought that this was a song about flowers. The tune was catchy, and after listening to her a while longer, I began to hum the tune softly to myself. I didn't pay much attention to the words.

I heard the song many times in the years that followed, and as I grew older I realized that it was not a song about flowers. It was a song about war.

As I grew older still, I began to wonder. I wondered how the girl on the bus, all those years ago, was able to sing that song with so much feeling. After all, the song was not her song. It belonged to the hippies, and to the communes, and to the protest marches and demonstrations against the war in Vietnam — but it did not belong to her. This was not her war. Her friends were not fighting in this war, nor were her brothers. So whence came this passion?

More years passed and I tried to leave my childhood behind me. I had become an adult, but something kept pulling me back, something that was terribly elusive and yet forcibly demanded my attention. I delved into my past and painfully peeled away the layers and layers that I had so deliberately built up to protect myself from myself. And when I finally reached the core of who I was, not only was I ready to take the final step into adulthood, but I had also found the answer to my other question, the question that began when I first heard that song.

For while it was true that this was not *her* war and therefore it was not her song, war was no stranger to that girl, nor was it to me. For both of our mothers and fathers had been in another war, a war so demented, a war so devoid of reason, that there were no songs written about it. And we, their children, could not sing of that war. We couldn't even talk about it — for nobody talked to us. But the passion of that war was there. It became part of us and we grew up with its demons inside us.

Now that our parents are finally beginning to talk, so, too, I feel it is time for us, their children, to talk and tell our story. This is my story.

CHAPTER ONE

THE MEMORY COMES to me today as if it had happened last night, and not on those long-ago nights of my early childhood. The piercing scream penetrating the darkness, the nameless rising terror as I was wrenched from the depths of slumber, the reverberating silence filled only with the wild pounding of my small heart...

I burrowed as far down in the blankets as I could, so that only the tips of my dark pigtails could still be seen above the covers. I huddled there for a long time listening to my heartbeats keeping rhythm to my uncontrolled shivering. When the closeness of the air began to suffocate me, I cautiously wiggled upwards until my head was once again resting on the pillow. The terror began to subside. Finally I heard only the soft murmuring of my parents' voices coming from the next room. This sound always followed the piercing scream.

I lay there, willing myself to fall asleep again, but as the early dawn light began to filter in through the white eyelet curtains, I became steadily more alert and began to gaze around my room. I tried to take comfort in my pleasant surroundings, allowing my eyes to linger on my white rocking horse, and then move over to gaze lovingly at my favorite doll. I watched the new day cast a warm glow on the rose-colored carpeting and the floral-patterned wallpaper. I saw the toys on my shelf take shape in the new light and my stuffed animals begin to emerge from their night's rest. Though my room was ideal for a four-year-old girl, I, as the sole occupant of this room, knew already at this tender age that the tale its decor and contents seemed to tell belonged in a book of fairy tales. The tale that had just been told by the sounds coming from the next room — that tale would have to be included in a book of truth.

At this time, though, aside from those nights when sleep was so disturbed and my days began with such fear, my life did borrow its pages from the world of fantasy.

I must start at the very beginning and bring my story to the present. For only by doing this can I explain my triumphs and my pain. Only by revealing those areas of my life that I have not felt comfortable sharing up till now, can I tell my story honestly.

I was born in Chicago, Illinois in 1950 when my mother was thirty-nine and my father was fifty years old. My parents, Sol and Faye Levy, had first met in Austria in 1937, but they had not been able to marry until 1945 when they arrived independently in the United States and had been reintroduced by a mutual relative. I was born five years later.

My parents brought me home from the hospital to a sprawling ranch-style house set well back from the road on three acres of property. They carried me to the room adjoining their bedroom which had just been converted to a nursery. They stood at the door hesitantly, as many new parents must. A sudden breeze ruffled the lacy pink skirt of the bassinet. They walked into the new nursery and gently placed me on my tummy on the soft white sheet. Then they stood back, gazing at me through tears that coursed down their cheeks. Neither could utter a sound, for the hysterical joy that filled them at that moment would, once unleashed, burst forth with such power that it would sing unrestrained forever.

After they had composed themselves somewhat, they retreated into the kitchen to eat for the first time on that memorable day. They hoped that they would finally be able to calm down enough to eat. It was already three o'clock in the afternoon and they knew that new parents, no matter how nervous, have to maintain their strength. They made sure to leave my door open so that they would be able to hear even the slightest whimper.

They debated my future over a hurriedly prepared meal of bread and scrambled eggs. They knew what they would name me; that was not a problem. I would be named for my grandmothers, both of whom were dead. One was called Chana Baila and the other was called Chana Rochel. My name would be Chana. But there were other questions. Would my mother stop helping my father in his office, or would they hire a babysitter to take care of me during those hours that she worked? Where would I go to school? What other outside lessons should they provide me with? And on and on the questions went, until the half-eaten eggs congealed into a lumpy yellow mass while I continued to sleep on, oblivious to all.

Most of their questions remained unanswered that afternoon, but the sheer joy of finally being able to discuss what concerned a child of their own more than made up for their lack of decisions. However, there was one decision that they agreed on immediately and unquestionably: this child would lack for nothing. All that they would have in their power to provide, regardless of effort or cost, she would have.

But what of that which was not in their power to provide?

CHAPTER TWO

WHETHER IT WAS DUE to my parents' determination to put my happiness before any other consideration, or to their unadulterated love for me, combined with their mature years; or whether it was actually due to any of the other myriad factors that conspire to provide well-being, my early childhood years were joyful ones. I was pretty and winsome enough to elicit smiles and pats on the head from even the most reserved adult, and my peers looked to me as their leader by the time I was five years old. My father, who at the time was receiving substantial royalties from an electronic device he had patented, considered nothing that money could buy to be too good for his only daughter. He constantly encouraged my mother to buy the newest toys and the latest in children's fashions. They would decorate and redecorate my room at least once a year. My house became the best place to play and all the neighborhood children incessantly nagged their mothers to take them there. All these children vied for my attention, and I dispensed it with élan.

I had it all. I had love, security, adulation, and wealth. What more could any child ask for?

Surprisingly enough, I did ask for more. For one thing,

I asked for fair weather all the time. The merest wisp of a cloud would threaten my happiness, and I'd get depressed if it rained.

And though I basked and frolicked in the sunshine most of the time, with my arms outstretched to embrace what the world had to offer and my head flung back to revel in the warmth of the sun, there were those times when I crouched with hunched shoulders, not daring to lift my head for fear of being pelted with cruel bullets of rain.

I have already described the terror of being awakened by a scream in the night. Those nights were unpredictable in their timing or frequency, but very predictable in the havoc which they wreaked on me. Even after the cold fingers of fear slackened their grip, I could not easily bounce back to my normal self. A tired numbness would wash over me and this lassitude would remain with me for the entire day. I would be too subdued to play with my friends, and would prefer looking at my picture books and dressing up my dolls. I was, of course, too young to realize how my mood on those days interacted with my parents' mood, causing them additional anguish.

There were other clouds on my horizon too. One, in particular, comes to mind for its perverse nature. My mother sang a lot. "So?" you might say. "Many people sing off-tune or have poor voices. What was the big deal?" But that wasn't it. My mother had a beautiful voice which could find the subtle tones of even the most complicated tune. Few things would bring my father and me more joy than to have my mother burst forth in the lively folk songs from "back home" or teach us some long-forgotten Yiddish ballad, or hum some current hit tune. It was at the other times — the times that I intuitively sensed that she was sad and disturbed by something — that I knew I was too young to understand. Then she would sing and the songs were long and plaintive. One was a Psalm, that my father said they had sung "in the camps," which I understood to mean in some sort of summer camp in Europe. I would silently steal away to my room, closing the door so that I could block out the haunting melodies. She herself would be too distracted to even notice that I had gone, for she too had been traveling to far and mysterious places, leaving me behind.

Then there was the confusion that I myself had helped to generate. One sunny Shabbos morning, when I was walking to shul with my mother, I turned to her and innocently asked the question that kids like to ask their parents: "Mommy, do you love me?"

She hesitated for a moment and then replied, "Oh, if I could only have twelve just like you!" I started to skip along gaily at her side, my black patent-leather shoes tapping the sidewalk. I swelled with pride, seeing myself multiplied twelve times. We all looked alike, were dressed alike, and smiled at each other with the same happy smile. Then, I suddenly sneaked a covert glance at my mother, and I was jolted out of my reverie. She did not look happy at all. There was a faraway look in her eyes and even a hint of tears. My skipping slowed to a shuffle and my eleven smiling, identical sisters all faded. What had happened? Why did my question evoke such pain?

Relentlessly, I used to bring up this question time and time again. I was hoping to understand my mother's reaction, but I was no wiser for all of my effort. Invariably, my mother would hesitate before answering, and offer me the same reply. And then I would sense that pervasive sadness. I am ashamed now of my persistence, but I have also come to understand why I could not leave this conversation alone.

It took me many years to perceive that regardless of how many friends I had over at my house and how much fun we had playing with my many toys and games, I was essentially a very lonely child. My mother's desire to have a dozen children fed into my own desire to have sisters and brothers. Other children had siblings. Why couldn't I?

When my friends went home at the end of the day, I

was left to my own devices. My father usually got home from work late, after I had gone to bed. My mother, though she tried hard to talk to me on these early evenings, was generally too tired to do more than sit on the couch and stab some stitches into a needlepoint tapestry.

I learned to read at an early age, and it was in books that I found comfort and a solution for my loneliness. I started off leafing through picture books, but before I had completed first grade I was already reading complete books on my own. My favorite ones were those written by Carolyn Haywood and Beverly Cleary: I loved getting to know Betsy and Eddie and Ramona. They were normal American children and they did normal American things. They got into pranks, took ballet lessons, and had watermelon parties. Their mothers always awaited their return home from school with smiles and plates of chocolate-chip cookies and tall glasses of milk.

I sometimes got into pranks, too. Once, when I had just discovered how to use the telephone, I called up the fire department. My mother had put the number on the bulletin board next to the phone. "Hello," I said. "We have a fire in our house."

"Is your mother home?" the voice on the other end asked.

"No, she went shopping," I replied, though my mother was outside, puttering in the garden. "I'm home all alone."

"Where is the fire?"

"In the kitchen," I said, "and it's getting bigger."

"Where do you live?"

I had just finished giving our address, which I had learned together with our phone number, when my mother walked in from the backyard, letting the screen door slam behind her.

"Who called?" she asked.

"Oh, I was just playing with the telephone," I answered innocently.

Three minutes later we heard the sirens come down our street. My mother hated the sound of sirens, and she would turn pale whenever she heard one. Not only that: when she heard ambulance sirens, she would check to make sure that my father and I were home. If we weren't, she'd call school or work to make sure that we were okay. In later years, I hated those calls. They embarrassed me, but I knew that I could not ask my mother not to make them. She felt compelled to make sure that we were safe.

Now, as the wailing sirens came to an abrupt halt in front of our house, my mother began to tremble uncontrollably. She ran to open the front door, and was surprised to see a shiny red fire engine pulling up at the curb. Two burly firemen jumped down from the truck and called out to her, "Is this the house with the fire in the kitchen?"

"Fire? What fire?" my mother asked, still shaking.

"Well, ma'am," the taller one said, "we got a call at the station saying that there was a fire at this address, and we came right over. Are you telling us that there is no fire?"

"I didn't call," my mother said in confusion. "Do you know who made the call?"

"No, ma'am — but it was a child's voice."

My mother looked over at me. By this time I was cowering behind the large leather recliner chair. One look and my mother knew that I was the guilty party. She was mortified. Apologizing for me, she promised the firemen that such an incident would never happen again. And then she dealt with me. Or rather, she didn't deal with me.

Had Betsy done the same thing in one of my books, her mother would have yelled at her or spanked her. Maybe she would have been sent to her room without supper. My mother did none of those things. She just looked at me, disappointment filling her eyes. And then she sighed and said, "Haven't I suffered enough? Why should my child do something like this? Wasn't I already punished for all of my sins?" She went to her room and closed the door. I had committed a crime that no Jewish girl had a right to commit. I was bad, bad, bad, and at that moment I hated myself more than anyone else could have possibly hated me. The prank was not worth the price.

I didn't fare any better when I dumped all of my dolls into the washing machine and added the contents of a whole box of detergent. My mother walked into the laundry room when the bubbles had begun to seep under the door. She found nothing amusing in seeing her daughter standing encased in a cloud of bubbles. Again, I had contributed to the suffering of one who was too fragile to endure any more aggravation.

Why did I do those things? I'm not exactly sure. Maybe these pranks were just the things that any child would do. Maybe I was just bored and I needed some stimulation. Or maybe I wanted to test my mother's love for me: Would she love me even if I were bad?

It's strange that I was insecure about her love. I certainly knew I was wanted. I always heard about how my parents had eagerly awaited my birth, and how thrilled they were to bring me home from the hospital. They were always buying me things — dresses, toys, and sweets. And they always took me along, wherever they want; other parents left their children with a babysitter. Most of the time, when I got home from school, my mother would open the front door and greet me with a big smile. But she wouldn't have any chocolate-chip cookies for me; I don't think she even knew what chocolate chips were! She would sit me down, though, and give me a big chunk of homemade yeast cake. She would cut me a piece from the middle of the cake, where the filling was thickest.

That was most of the time. But there were other days as well, days when the picture didn't look at all like my favorite books. On those days I would come home from school and there would be no one to greet me. With a tightness in my throat I would let myself into the silent house, where I would find my mother stretched out on the couch with a cold compress over her eyes. She would murmur from her prone position, "Chanie, is that you?" That was all she would say for the remainder of the afternoon. She would continue to lie there, immobilized by her headache. I knew not to make any noise. I couldn't have any friends over. I couldn't play any of my records and I couldn't even open the refrigerator to help myself to a snack. The noise made by the opening and closing of the refrigerator door was liable to set off a cry of agony. On those days my mother probably wanted me to go out and play in the backyard, but I was afraid to leave the house. I didn't know what I would find when I got back, and that fear kept me rooted to the house, close to my mother. I had to protect her, although from what, I wasn't sure. Maybe it was this role reversal that made me insecure.

Possibly it was something else altogether, though. Sometimes, I sat with my mother and she would tell me about the family I had never met...and would never meet. She would talk about her brothers and her sisters, her parents and her grandparents, and about her aunts and uncles. I remember that once, when I was very little, I asked her what aunts and uncles were. She sighed. "An aunt is your mother's or father's sister, and an uncle is your mother's or father's brother."

"Where are my aunts and uncles?" I asked. "Where do they live?"

"You don't have any aunts and uncles."

"Why not? But you just told me about your sisters and brothers — aren't they my aunts and uncles? And doesn't Tatty have sisters and brothers? Aren't they my aunts and uncles, too?"

"Well, yes, they would be..." My mother's voice was strained, but she was trying to keep it steady. "...If they were alive, but..."

"But what?" I demanded. "Where are they? What happened to them? And why haven't I ever seen my grandparents? My Zaidie and my Bubbie? You had grandparents.

Where are my grandparents?"

My mother didn't answer me right away. Her face assumed the same closed and distant look that it wore when she sang her sad songs. I sat very still at her side, not daring to interrupt her musing. The passing of the minutes was marked by the ticking of the old grandfather clock in the hall.

Finally my mother turned and gazed down at me. "Chanie, it's a long, long story. You're too little to understand it. You did have grandparents, and you did have aunts and uncles. But they're not... they're not living anymore. May God avenge their blood." She drew a shaky breath. "But you do have us, your Mommy and your Tatty. You're very lucky. You have a Mommy and a Tatty. And we have *you*. We're very lucky, too. Oh, Chanie, if you only knew what it is to have a Tatty and a Mommy, how happy you would be!" She closed her eyes and the tears streamed down her cheeks. "How I would love to have my Mommy and my Tatty!" I put my little hand into her big one. I squeezed very hard, so that she would feel that she had me. "When you were born," she continued, "we named you after your grandmothers. You are them, and they are you."

I didn't understand most of what she said. It was all very confusing. Once upon a time there had apparently been a lot of people who were all relatives. Something had happened to them. My mother wouldn't tell me what, but it was something very bad. But there was also something very good. That something was connected to my mother and my father and me. Then there was something else, and I didn't know if it was good or bad: It had to do with grandmothers and grandfathers and aunts and uncles and how I was a part of them and they were a part of me. But what did that mean? How could I be me and them? Was I Chana Me or was I Chana Them? And did my parents love me because I was their child, or did they really love me because I was named for their mothers?

There were more clouds during those early years, but they played a game of hide-and-seek. I would no sooner spot them and try to identify them, than they would blow past and disappear, only to reappear and catch me unawares some time later. In those years my perception was too shallow and my thought patterns too undeveloped to really recognize and catalog them properly.

CHAPTER THREE

MY SCHOOL YEARS followed the same pattern. They were, for the most part, happy years. I would merrily set out for school each morning with my neatly-packed briefcase and my brown-bagged lunch, complete with the special treat that my mother never forgot to include, clutched in my hand. I would be joined on the way by two of my best friends and together we would all arrive at school a couple of minutes before the bell rang.

The classes were easy for me. I found that if I listened intently during the first few minutes of class, and then tuned in for the last few minutes of review at the end, I could usually indulge in daydreaming or reading a book for my own pleasure during most of the period. Tests were more of a game than a source of tension. Math was the only subject I ever had trouble with, and it's a good thing I did, for I would surely not have been able to relate to some of my friends' misery in class had it not been for my own trouble.

Then there was recess, the highlight of the morning and the highlight of the afternoon. Having always been the leader of my peers even during my preschool years, I quite naturally assumed that role as soon as I started attending school. I called the shots, deciding which games we would play, who would belong to which team, and even when we would choose to ignore the bell that called us back to class.

I would like to think that I was always fair and kind to my classmates, from my position of power, but my memory tells me that this was not the case. I remember some kids even crying when they felt left out, but then, of course, it would always be me who would rush to their sides and comfort them. I would always feel quite noble after one of these episodes. Even though I may have inadvertently helped cause their distress, I certainly went all out to make them feel better. As far as I was concerned, all was well that ended well. I didn't bother to analyze how humiliated these kids must have felt to have the class witness their tears, or how their egos may have felt bruised long after they smiled at me with forgiveness. But how could I really understand the position of the underdog? A person standing at the top of the world has trouble perceiving a person at the bottom as more than a mere speck. Basically, it took a tumble to the bottom to correct my myopia. But this did not happen until many years later.

The more entrenched I became in my position of leadership, the more fearful I became of losing it. I did not dare do anything that might jeopardize my position, but the price I paid for maintaining it was a steep one.

As a young child, I had no need for an intense friendship. Friends were people with whom I shared toys, games, jokes, and laughter — no more and no less. But as I began my school years, such superficial friendship was not enough. I longed for somebody with whom I could share my thoughts and dreams, a true best friend to confide in as well as have fun with. No one in school would do, for I would not expose my needs to any of my classmates. I was afraid that if they discovered my vulnerability, I would lose the prestige that I so valued. Now my loneliness at home was exacerbated by my growing loneliness in school. I wonder if eventually I would have learned that a leader can reveal her vulnerability and still remain, and be considered a better, leader. Or even if not, that leadership was not worth the price of a good friendship. However, I did not have to choose between the two.

One warm day in late spring, when I was ten years old, I was sprawled on the lawn under our giant maple tree, engrossed in rereading one of my favorite books, when I heard a large truck come rumbling down the street. I looked up from my book and saw a moving van which was followed by a yellow station wagon. Both vehicles came to a halt at the curb across the street, in front of the house that had been put up for sale two months before.

Three sets of doors were flung open at once. At first I was captivated by the actions of the two truckers who began to unload the contents of the van. But then I caught sight of a girl emerging from the car, a girl who looked as though she had stepped off the pages of my book. She had straight blond hair, a pert little nose with freckles sprinkled across its bridge, and wide green eyes. She was wearing blue shorts and a red T-shirt. She seemed to be about my age. She followed the man, the woman, and a little boy across the threshold of the house. I was disappointed to see that both the man and the boy were bare-headed. I had hoped that my new neighbors would be Jewish.

I put down my book, jumped up, and went over to introduce myself. I knocked on the open door and the girl appeared.

"Hi, I'm Chanie," I said. "I live across the street. It's okay if you can't say 'Chanie.' It's a Jewish name and it's kind of hard to pronounce. You can call me Connie if you want. My English teachers in school do. What's your name?"

"My name is Marjorie. And of course I can say 'Chanie'! We're Jewish, too."

"You are?" I asked in surprise. "You don't look it," I blurted tactlessly.

"What do you mean, I don't look it?" Marjorie said, flushing. "We keep Shabbos and eat kosher! I'm just as Jewish are you are."

Realizing that my hopes for a new friendship had gotten off to a bad start, I changed the subject. "How old are you?" I asked.

"Nine," Marjorie replied. "How old are you?"

"I'm ten. I'm in fifth grade. What grade are you in?"

"I'm in fourth grade. What school do you go to? I'm going to be at Hillel."

"Well, I go to Bais Yaakov. How come you're not going there? It's only three blocks away."

"Hillel is better," Marjorie explained. "I heard my father tell my mother that."

"It is not! My mother says that Bais Yaakov is the best school in the whole world," I exaggerated. My chances for making a new friend seemed to be going from bad to worse!

I tried again. "Do you want to come over to my house? I have lots of toys."

"Okay. Let me ask my mother."

With permission granted, Marjorie spent the afternoon at my house. We didn't have any more arguments that day and I knew that I had found a friend. While we were playing, my mother baked a cake for the new neighbors, and she took it over to their house while it was still warm. She must have spent some time getting to know them, because I noticed that she didn't come home for a full half-hour.

After my parents had tucked me in for the night, they sat down to talk. I couldn't fall asleep right away because I was so excited about my new friend, but my parents assumed that I had fallen asleep as fast as I usually did. They didn't bother to lower their voices, and though I did not understand everything they said, I heard it all quite clearly.

"You know that house that was for sale across the street?" my mother began. "Well, a new family just moved in — their name is White."

"White?" my father asked. "What kind of people are they?"

"They seem to be very nice. They have a daughter who's Chanie's age, and a boy a couple of years younger. I'm really happy for Chanie — she's seemed a bit lonely lately."

"Are they Jewish?" my father wanted to know.

"Not only are they Jewish," my mother replied, "but they're even *shomer Shabbos.*"

"Oh, that's good. So the girl will probably to go school with Chanie."

"No. That's the funny part," my mother said. "I was surprised to find out that they keep Shabbos — they don't even look Jewish! The father looks real American and he didn't have a yarmulke on, and neither did the boy. The mother looks just like a fashion model, and how she managed to do that on moving day is anybody's guess. And listen to this: they have two television sets, and I saw an American flag curled up in the corner. If not for the fact that the father has a heavy accent, I wouldn't believe that they could be anything but blue-blooded Americans."

My mother seemed a little too excited, almost agitated, and my father was very quiet. I strained to hear something that would explain the feeling of foreboding I sensed. It was coming.

"We got to talking about schools and I told him that Chanie goes to Bais Yaakov, and wouldn't it be nice for both of the girls if they could go to the same school. As soon as I mentioned Bais Yaakov, Mr. White got very upset. 'No daughter of mine is going to that kind of school!' he said."

I could imagine my father raising his gray, bushy eyebrows and waiting for my mother to continue. "I asked him what he meant by that and in reply he rolled up his sleeve. 'See that?' he said, pointing to the numbers tattooed on his arm. (Here, I think, my father said "Ah-h.") 'That's what happens when everyone knows you're Jewish. They come and get you. They may have been nice to you all along, but, believe me, one day they just come and get you. That's what happened to me, but it's not going to happen to my family. No, no, it's not going to happen to them. Once was enough. Never again. My family is not going to walk around looking Jewish, just begging to be rounded up like a herd of cattle. We're a good Jewish family, but we keep our Jewishness at home. We keep Shabbos and we keep kosher and we pray. And my daughter will go to a Jewish school, but not one that's going to make her walk around dressed like she still lives in the *shtetl.* You can have your Bais Yaakov with its long dresses and its stockings. My daughter is going to look like every other American kid. I'm not looking for trouble.'"

I heard my father sigh, and say something softly. Then my mother went on, and what she said suddenly sounded loud to me. "I showed him that I, too, have a tattoo. I tried to explain to him that it is our Jewishness that would protect us if..."

But I had stopped listening. When my mother said that word, that terrible and strange word — *tattoo* — I was enveloped in a cloud of fear. I had once asked her about it, but she didn't answer me. I tried to recall the numbers of her tattoo, but my mind went blank. I forced myself to concentrate and I did seem to remember an *A* and perhaps there was a *3* and maybe a *1*. I wasn't sure. I had never felt comfortable looking at it. My mother had dressed me with that arm and fed me with that arm, but somehow I knew not to stare at it. I wondered if Marjorie knew the number on her father's arm. I decided to ask her about it when I had a chance, and then I fell asleep.

School, too, had its clouds. They were even more infrequent than those at home, but the combined picture could sometimes allude to a sinister storm.

Most schools had young, American-born teachers whose very presence evoked images of polished apples, lavender-scented hankies, and smooth, unbroken pieces of chalk.

They taught kids who came from American homes where English was the only spoken language, chocolate-chip cookies were the favorite snack, and Mom and Dad had cheerful, unlined faces.

My school also had American teachers. They taught us secular subjects in the afternoons. They introduced us to the three R's, opened our minds to the sciences, and whetted our appetites to explore the world around us. They had nice smiles, even temperaments, and clear skin that hinted at Ivory soap.

It was the morning teachers, though, who were more familiar to us. They looked and sounded like our parents. They tended to wear conservative clothes whose cut could not disguise the stooped shoulders and knobby joints of their owners. When the weather was hot and they would roll up their sleeves, they would also reveal their membership in the club: Their numbers were engraved forever on their forearms, in indelible blue ink.

These teachers dispensed smiles as if each one would set them back a month's salary. Bouts of teaching would alternate with unexplained sighs, silences, and faraway looks, broken only with whispered cries of "*Oy vay, oy vay.*" Their wrinkled faces proclaimed them to be at least twice as old as our afternoon teachers, but that was not so.

While our afternoon sessions were co-ed, in the mornings the boys and girls would be taught separately. We girls got the better part of the deal. Our teachers may not have been young, carefree, and peppy, but they were devoted and compassionate. We sensed their love for us and we knew that they took the mission of educating us very seriously. The boys had a much harder time. Their teachers had trouble relating to them and were greatly vexed by their antics and restlessness. The boys' teachers were irritated by their casual approach to learning and did not have the patience to deal with them. Who can blame them for not understanding their young charges, when they themselves had been so cruelly deprived of their own youth?

Once or twice a year, our mornings would also include "story hour" — but not the usual kind. Not the nice tame activity where all the children get comfortably settled around the teacher and allow her soothing voice to lull them as she spins her tales and takes pleasure in exposing her charges to good, classic, children's literature. No, not these kinds of stories! Our stories were unsurpassed in their horror, and told the terrible tale of what had happened not so many years before. I could not dismiss them as fiction. I would sit for the remainder of the day with clammy hands and nausea, unable to concentrate in class. I wouldn't even be able to go out for recess. I would watch the clock and as soon as the final bell rang, I would dash home to confront my mother with a recital of the horror story, and I would beg her to tell me that it wasn't true, that it couldn't be, that such things couldn't happen, didn't happen.

But she didn't reassure me. She couldn't. All the color would leave her face and a shudder would pass through her. She would collapse on the couch and would leave me far behind as she traveled once more away from me and back into some awful point in time. Though I knew that I should not persist in my questioning, I was so upset by what I'd heard, so disturbed by her secrecy, that I would sometimes continue to question her after she had returned to me. She would shake her head from side to side, and say, "No, no, Chanie...no, I cannot...you are too young...I want you to be happy...you must be happy...you are my only...please, please, no..."

CHAPTER FOUR

DURING MY HIGH-SCHOOL years, the ever-threatening clouds began to clear a little. Much of this was due to the perceptiveness I gained as I grew older, as well as my parents' understanding of my new maturity. I now knew when it was a time to question and when it was a time to keep quiet. At the same time, my parents were not quite so reticent in my presence. While they still kept their vow of silence concerning the actual horrors they had witnessed or experienced under the Nazis, they were more willing to explain to me why they were the way they were.

When I complained about the supper menu or when I did not finish all that was on my plate, now they would do more than just look offended: my mother would tell me it hurt her to see good food wasted because she had endured so many years of relentless hunger. My father would nod in agreement, and together they would encourage me to eat just a little bit more.

Before, whenever we had visitors whose arms were also tattooed with digits, my parents would quickly switch to a European language that I couldn't understand when the "*lager*" was the topic of discussion; now, they would glance in my direction, make sure that I was absorbed in my book, and continue the conversation in Yiddish, which they knew I understood. I would simply pretend that I wasn't paying any attention, and in this way, I gleaned enough information to put together some picture of the life my parents had led during their horror-filled youth.

I began to understand their intensity, their almost frantic reaction to even the most subtle nuance of joy or pain. Their shrill laughter, their ready tears, and their exaggerated body language no longer mystified me. They had learned, in the most bizarre fashion, that nothing in life could be trusted. So they grabbed each moment, lived it to the fullest, and thereby tried to keep the fear at bay that they could once again be robbed of everything.

I also began to understand why my mother insisted that she wanted "twelve just like me," and why that desire brought her so much pain. She knew that she was too old to have any more children, yet she bore the onus to replace her eleven siblings: her own beloved parents had once had "twelve just like me," all but one of whom had died in the cruelest massacre of all ages.

I learned to accept my parents' refusal to allow me to sleep away from home, walk home late at night, or go on the wild rides at amusement parks. How could my desire for a good time supersede my parents' crushing fear that something might happen to their "one and only"?

My new knowledge burdened me with new responsibilities which I had to exchange for the frivolity of my younger years. Thus began my emergence into adulthood.

Some of my friends came from backgrounds that were similar to mine. Strangely, though, we did not have any particular allegiance to each other; if anything, we all tended to be attracted to the most "American" element in our class. Perhaps we hoped that our association with those happy-go-lucky girls who came from carefree homes would lighten or dilute our own intensity.

I had become quite friendly with Esther. Esther was a

wholesome girl with apple-red cheeks and an athletic build. She had a resounding voice and an infectious laugh. And most amazing of all, not only were her parents American, but even her grandparents had been born in America! One set of grandparents lived a couple of blocks away from them, and the other set lived in Denver, Colorado.

The Denver grandparents would fly in to visit two or three times a year. Sometimes they came alone and at other times Esther's aunt and uncle and her three cousins would accompany them. Every other year the whole clan would gather at Esther's house for Passover and the table would be extended with three leaves, to accommodate the (similarly) extended family. Though the house would become crowded with people, luggage, and sleeping bags, I would always try to visit Esther during those times. It gave me a vicarious thrill to imagine what it would be like to be part of her family. I could see myself snuggling into one of the sleeping bags with a cousin my own age, giggling and sharing confidences late into the night. I would envision her kindly grandfather hobbling into the room and — in all-American unaccented English — reprimanding us with mock seriousness for disturbing his sleep. I could picture her plump little grandmother coming in to join him and insisting that since we were all up anyway, we might as well go into the kitchen to have some of her special Passover cake.

Esther visited my house often too. She would come over to study whenever we had a major test scheduled for the next day. At her house there was always so much going on that it was impossible to study. My house was quiet. I liked to have her over, and my parents also enjoyed her company — her bubbly personality did a lot to lighten the somber mood that prevailed in our home.

One day Esther dropped by unexpectedly. This was not unusual, for we had taken to visiting each other quite frequently. But this time she picked the wrong day to pop in unannounced. The night before, my mother had lit the candle.

Americans associate candles with happy occasions. Ask any American in what setting candles are used. They will surely tell you that candles go with the scent of roses and soft piano music. Their eyes will turn dreamy as they imagine themselves seated at a candle-lit table, dining on exquisitely prepared food served on the best china and silver.

But ask any Jewish child of Holocaust survivors to tell you what they associate candles with, and the first thing they will tell you is that candles are lit by a mother to bless the Sabbath and to pour out her heart to God. The lighting of candles is a time for tears and prayers. If you dare to question them further, they will tell you something more, that candles are used to commemorate the anniversary of a death. But they will not tell you that nothing else can mark this day. There are no flowers to take to the cemetery, for there are no graves. Their eyes will become haunted as they imagine a body going up in flames. It would be too painful to tell you this and you would not understand.

Esther came over that day to borrow a book. We were in ninth grade and had lots of book reports to do that year. We had one due the next day, and, since Esther tended to do her homework at the last minute, she hadn't even read a book yet. So she came over to see if I had a book that she could borrow.

She flung her bike down on the lawn as usual and came bouncing up to the house. She merrily pushed the bell three times, and then shouted, "Is anyone home?"

I rushed to answer the door. My mother was lying on the couch with one of her headaches, and Esther had never seen her that way. I blocked Esther's view of her by ushering her quickly into the kitchen. And there was the candle burning in its glass, flickering and casting its shadows over the walls of the kitchen.

"Listen, Esther, maybe we'll go outside and talk," I said quickly.

Esther looked at me as if I were crazy. "Go outside!?" Workmen were repairing the sewer system and they were busy excavating a deep ditch. There were clods of sticky red clay flung across the lawn and the smell of rotting sewage permeated the yard and even seeped into the house a little. The noise of the bulldozer competed with the clang of the pipes. "Into that mess and that horrible smell?" she went on. "And how can we hear each other through that awful racket?"

My heart was pounding. I nodded and turned to lead us to my bedroom so that we could escape the ominous presence of the flickering candle. But then I remembered that we would have to pass by my mother on the way. I bumped clumsily into Esther as I turned suddenly and did an about-face.

"Let's sit here," I said, trying to keep my voice "normal," and I resignedly sat down at the kitchen table.

It didn't take Esther long to ask the question that I was dreading. "Oh, whose *yahrtzeit* is it?"

I did not know what to answer. Should I tell her it was the *yahrtzeit* of my mother's father, her brother Berel, her brother Mordechai, and her brother Eli? No, I couldn't. That would just lead to more questions. She would want to know how come they all had the same *yahrtzeit* and I, myself, was not too sure of the answer.

Instead of answering, I busied myself with slicing us some cake and putting it on the table, with a bottle of milk and some cups and napkins.

Esther filled the silence with talk of her own family. "You know, my great-grandfather's *yahrtzeit* is on the fourth day of Passover. He came here from Russia at the turn of the century, when he was only ten years old, and he managed to stay religious while growing up in America — which at the time was quite a feat, I understand. Of course, he was already an old man by the time I was born, but I still remember sitting on his lap while he told me stories of the way it was. He would tell me about the challenges he faced in America and how he never desecrated the Sabbath, even during the Depression."

I nodded, and gazed at the *yahrtzeit* shadows dancing on the wall while I listened to Esther's cheerful voice.

"We all go to visit his grave together when my grandparents come in for Passover. It works out well because all of us kids are off from school and our parents usually try to take off from work, too. However, in a way it's kind of tough having the *yahrtzeit* come out on Passover — it's our custom to serve cake and drinks after the morning prayers on the day of the *yahrtzeit*, and my mom can't bake her regular cakes on Passover!"

Esther paused long enough for me to mull over her words. I had never viewed a *yahrtzeit* as a time for a family get-together. How could I? There was no family. No *we* and no *all*. And as for it being tough to have the *yahrtzeit* come out on Passover — well, some things were a lot tougher.

I caught Esther glancing again at the candle and I realized that I hadn't answered her question. What was I to say?

I had never discussed the *yahrtzeit* candle with anyone, not even my parents. When they were lighting it, I would walk out of the room. I would still hear their sobbing, but I did not want to embarrass them by watching them cry. The whole time the candle burned, I would be very good. I never invited any friends over on those days. I would play quietly with my puzzles or read a book. I felt very lonely. Sometime during the course of the day, I would go over and sit beside the parent who had lit the candle. I would move over as closely as I could, so that our bodies would touch. I wanted them to know that at least they had me.

I could not tell any of this to Esther. I didn't have the words to express what those days meant to me or what they meant to my parents. And even if I had had the words, I would not have felt comfortable revealing myself in that way. My parents never talked and neither did I.

While I was wondering how to respond to Esther's question, my mother passed by the door to the kitchen. Esther couldn't see her because she was facing the other way. I tensed up, wondering how to stop Esther's cheerful babbling before my mother heard her, for I knew that Esther's very presence would be jarring to her. I knew, too, that if Esther were to innocently question my mother the way she had questioned me, my mother would suffer great anguish. I had to protect her.

I had been trying to protect my parents from pain my whole life. Even before I had a clue about what they had been through, I knew that it was a big sin to hurt them. They never told me so, but I knew it anyway. I learned the rule of "Honor thy father and mother" in school, but I was well-versed in its meaning even before I started school. And now that I knew a bit more, I was even more careful not to hurt them. Sometimes, I felt like a mother to my parents. And as a mother, my sense of danger was aroused. I knew that Esther's chatter would hurt my mother deeply.

I tried motioning to my mother that I would come to her in a moment, but Esther caught my gesture and turned around to see my mother. "Oh, hi, Mrs. Levy!" she said brightly. My mother stepped into the kitchen from the dim hallway. In the fluorescent light, Esther was able to see that my mother wasn't well. The eerie light of the candle didn't help. "Aren't you feeling okay today?"

My mother avoided answering Esther's question and said to her instead, "It's good to see you, Esther. You haven't been around for a while. Were you and Chanie planning to do something today?" Her usually strong voice was faint now.

"Well, really I should be working on my book report. But when I came over to borrow the book, we got to talking. I thought that maybe if I started to work on it over here, I could get it done quickly. Would I be in your way?"

My mother and I exchanged glances. Neither of us looked too happy.

"Esther," my mother said to her, "maybe this is not the best place to do your homework today. What with all the noise from the construction, I got a slight headache and though you know you're always welcome, I'm afraid that I'm not really up to any company. Would you mind very much working on your report at home today?"

"Oh, no, not at all, Mrs. Levy. That's fine. Would you like me to make you a cup of tea? Do you want me to run to the drug store and get some aspirin?"

"No, Esther, but thanks for offering. It's very sweet of you. But I think that all I need is some quiet, so if you'll excuse me, I'll go back and lie down."

My mother left the room and Esther turned back to me, waiting for an explanation. I had none to offer her, so I didn't say anything. I was feeling very down and Esther's bubbly chatter was beginning to grate on me. She was in one world and I was in another. "Esther," I said, "there's something I wanted to take care of today and I was kind of counting on this afternoon to get it done, so if you don't mind..."

"It's okay, Chanie, I can take a hint!" she replied good-naturedly. "I'm on my way."

It wasn't till after Esther left that I realized just how upset I was. I had always found the *yahrtzeit* days very unsettling, but I had accepted them as part of my life, in the way that death, in general, is accepted by everyone as a part of life. But now Esther's words made me question this acceptance.

Imagine taking a *yahrtzeit* candle for granted! Imagine having four grandparents! Imagine remembering your grandfather's father! And even knowing anything about his life! Imagine having parents who were young and carefree and spoke without an accent! But whose life was the normal one, mine or Esther's? The question went round and round in my head and I knew that I had to talk with someone. Should I ask my parents? No, I couldn't do that. They would think that they had made me unhappy in some way, and that would hurt them. I couldn't talk to any of my friends at school. Some of them, I knew, would understand me. Their parents were also European and they probably had the same questions I had. But we all adhered to our parents' vow of silence, and I was not going to be the one to break it. There was only one person I could talk to.

I picked out a couple of books from the shelves in my room, and told my mother that Esther had forgotten to take a book for her report and that I was going to drop it off. She nodded from her position on the couch and I closed the door gently behind me.

Dropping off the book was just an excuse to leave the house, but since I didn't want to lie, I first stopped off at Esther's house and left the books with one of her sisters. Then I doubled back to my own block and went over to Marjorie.

Marjorie was in the backyard clearing up the remains of the barbecue supper they'd had. The smell of smoke filled the air and it nauseated me. I turned away from the scorched bones that were lying in a heap in the middle of the picnic table.

"Hi, Chanie," she said as she threw an empty Coke bottle into the garbage. "I tried to call you a few times today, but I kept getting a busy signal."

"Yeah, I know. My mother had a terrible headache, so she took the phone off the hook. I really feel bad for her. She gets these headaches at least once a week." I paused, not sure how to continue. Then I blurted out, "I've noticed that your father gets headaches, too."

"Yes, he does. He's gone to a lot of doctors to try and find the cause. Each of them took a bunch of tests, which all came out negative. They gave him some prescriptions and then told him that the headaches were due to stress. That upset my father very much. He's proud of himself for always being in control and he views these headaches as a sign of weakness. He doesn't even mention it when he has a headache anymore, unless it's really bad. But we can tell, and obviously you can, too."

"Well, I guess I can tell because his skin turns the same color as my mother's does. And they both have the same way of putting their fingers against their temples. I wonder if they both have headaches for the same reason."

"What do you mean?"

Somehow the torrent of words poured out. "To tell you the truth, Marjorie, there was something that I wanted to ask you about four years ago, but I was afraid that you wouldn't know what I was talking about. I guess by now, though, you probably will. On the day you moved in, my mother said something about the number that your father has on his arm. I'm sure you've noticed that my mother has one too." Marjorie nodded, her clear green eyes looking serious. "On that day," I went on, my voice getting stronger, "I tried to remember my mother's number and I discovered that I just couldn't remember a single digit for sure. Do you know what that number means, Marjorie, and do you know what your father's number is?"

Marjorie was not used to seeing me so intense, and she looked surprised. "Do I know what his number is?" she echoed, ignoring the first part of my question. "Um, let me think a minute. Let's see. It starts with a letter, I think. Wait. Maybe it's a number. No, that's strange. I've looked at his arm at least a thousand times, but no — I can't remember the number!"

"Why, Marjorie? Why do you think that is?"

Maybe my strange mood was catching, for Marjorie began to talk now too, her words coming as rapidly as mine had. "To tell you the truth, Chanie, I don't really know. I don't like to think about it much. I know my father was in some sort of camp and he got the number there, but I don't know much more. Whenever I try to ask him anything about the time before I was born, he just tells me to leave him alone. He changes the subject and starts giving me a whole big speech about what a great place America is. He tells me that I'm very lucky to have been born in America. My father is more patriotic than anyone I know.

"And sometimes when I come home from your house and ask my mother if she could get some recipes from your mother, my father interrupts and says, 'That's not American food.' Now what's wrong with eating European food? My father insists that my brother wear jeans to school even though he hates them. We spend almost every Sunday touring national parks and landmarks. I find it very boring, but my father says that it's all part of becoming a good citizen. He makes me and my brother read books on American history and I have a hard enough time sitting through history class in school! He wants us to be super-American, but I don't really know why. My mother seems to agree with him, although she doesn't explain it either. I just know that it has something to do with his childhood." She smiled. "I guess our homes are very different, Chanie!"

"Uh, uh, Marjorie. They're not different at all."

"How can you say that? Your house is so European, and mine is so American!"

"Well, let me ask you something, Marjorie," I said. I stopped to wipe my face with a tissue from my pocket. I tightened my pony tail. The evening was cold but I was burning up. "Better yet, let me ask you a few things. You don't have to answer me if you don't want to. I've never asked anyone else these questions, but they're beginning to choke me." I leaned closer. "Listen — do you ever see your parents cry? Do they ever scream in the middle of the night? Do you ever hear them laughing? I mean like *really* laughing, as though they were really enjoying themselves?"

Marjorie looked away, her face pale in the darkening twilight. "I...I don't want to answer your first two questions. I don't think it would be fair to my parents for me to discuss those things with you. But as for laughing, that makes me curious, too. I do hear them laugh sometimes. They'll laugh at a good joke or if my brother or I do something funny. But they laugh and kind of like hold it back at the same time. I'm not sure how to explain it. It's sort of like they begin to laugh and then they change their mind. Like they're about to do something awful or something. I feel bad about it. They never look like they're having a good time, but they keep telling me to have a good time. They even yell at me when I'm upset about something. It's sort of like, 'Do as I say, not as I do'."

"Oh, that's just what I mean, Marjorie. My parents are the same way! It's like they have a monopoly on suffering and they want me to have a monopoly on happiness. It's almost as if they took the emotional pie and divided it down the middle. They finished the half with suffering sandwiched between the crusts, and now they want me to finish the half with the happiness sandwiched inside. But when I look at them and I know that they have suffered, I feel that maybe I don't deserve to be happy. I'm not a better person than they are. On the contrary, they're much better people than I can ever hope to be." I was amazed at myself. Vague feelings that had been with me for much of my fourteen years suddenly spilled out as fully-formed sentences. "Sometimes I even think that maybe it's just a matter of time till I'll have to suffer, too, like they did. It's scary."

"It is," said Marjorie. "But I don't like to think about it. It's hard to sort of get hold of the thought..."

"I don't like to think about it much either, but lately I'm finding it harder and harder to ignore. You know my friend Esther? She came over today to borrow a book. My mother had a *yahrtzeit* — that's why she had a headache, I guess.

Anyway, Esther came bouncing in and started to ask me questions about whose *yahrtzeit* it was. I couldn't believe that she could ask such a personal question so casually. Then I realized that for *her*, a *yahrtzeit* is no big deal. Her grandparents are still alive, and so are all her aunts and uncles! Only old people in her family have died. So what's the big deal?

"That got me to thinking about her home. Now, that's a home that's *really* different from ours. Her parents have a lot of fun with their kids. They yell at them a lot, too, but then it blows over very quickly. And when they laugh, they *laugh*. You know, her father shakes when he laughs! And her mother's always so happy and peaceful. There's always a kid hanging onto her skirt and crying — the noise in that house is deafening! And what does her mother do? She puts on a record and sings loud enough to drown out all the rest of the noise! And just imagine — she never has any headaches!"

I called home and my mother must have been feeling better because the receiver had been put back on. I told her I was at Marjorie's. Marjorie and I spent the rest of the evening comparing notes about our families. For me it was a catharsis. And not only did it become clear to Marjorie that our homes were very similar, but I also realized that there were even more similarities than I had first thought. By the end of the evening, I was a lot more at peace with myself than I'd been for ages. I had always harbored a secret fear that no one thought the thoughts I thought. Maybe that's why I was always afraid to open up to anyone: if they knew the real me, they might reject me. Now I had finally confided in someone, and it felt good. I understood myself better, I understood my friend better, and I resolved that I would now try to understand my parents better as well. I decided that I would gather as much information as I could about the horrors that they had experienced, from any source that would offer it.

School helped to fill in some of the gaps in my knowledge left over from any eavesdropping at home. As we matured, our teachers broadened our horizons about the World War II era with historical data as well as the course of anti-Semitism throughout our existence as a nation. We were shocked to learn that cruelty to the Jews was as old as the Jewish People itself, and we were even more shocked to learn how diabolical was the will to exterminate us. In this area, Man used his gift of reason to surpass even the most ferocious beast in his convoluted plans to torment and annihilate us. These tactics reached a finely-honed perfection under the Nazi regime.

Reading also helped to satisfy my need for information. Unfortunately, in the sixties very little about the Jews' view of the Nazi era had been recorded. Apparently, my parents were not the only ones who were afraid to open the floodgates of their memories. The majority of the former camp inmates joined them in their vow of silence. I had to resort to the fictionalized accounts of those years, books such as those written by Leon Uris, where at least I had the luxury of convincing myself, when the reading got too rough, that it was all make-believe anyway, and of course these horrible anecdotes could not have happened in real life. Later, I was to discover that the truth far surpassed the fiction in actual horror. It was while reading one of these books that an obscure, almost-forgotten memory of my early childhood also became clear.

My father had asked me to bring him a handkerchief from his chest of drawers. I opened up the drawer and began shuffling through the handkerchiefs in order to pick the crispest one. Suddenly a strange-looking little black book caught my eye. As I reached into the drawer to pull it out so that I could examine it further, my hand encountered an even stranger object: It was a little flesh-colored rectangle encased in a creased piece of plastic. The handkerchief was forgotten as I raced into the kitchen to show my father what

I had found. He blanched when he saw what I was waving in my hand.

"Put it back!" he yelled in a voice he had never used with me before.

"But what is it, Tatty?" I cried.

"Just put it back," he repeated as bright red and purple splotches appeared on the pallor of his face.

"But why?" I insisted. "Just tell me what it is and I'll put it back right away."

"It's soap," he said hoarsely. "Now put it right back where you found it."

"Soap? Can I wash with it?" I asked.

"No, no, no!" And as he shakily rose from his chair, I knew that once again I had pushed too far. Even more perplexed than when I had first found the offending object, I ran out of the room and tossed the soap into a back corner in the bottom of the drawer.

There it remained, not even to reemerge in my memory, until I read of the cannibalism of the Nazi beast. "Waste not, want not" must have been their motto as they stuffed their victims' hair into mattresses, wove their skin into lampshades, and boiled their fat down into bars of soap.

I stared at the printed words and the book fell from my hands, as I burst into hysterical sobbing. So that was the story behind the soap. I buried my head in the pillow so that my parents would not come to investigate why I was crying. Though I needed their comfort, I knew that I had caused them enough pain. I owed them the right to leave their memories undisturbed.

CHAPTER FIVE

THAT WAS THE DARKER SIDE of my adolescent and teen years. While it occupied my subconscious mind like an insidious cancer, it actually played a very minor role in my daily life. I was just a girl who wanted to have fun, and that's exactly what I did.

Upper-class learning came easily to me, with the exception of math, of course. So aside from having to work a little harder over algebra and geometry, I had plenty of time to fully enjoy the social scene. I was voted class president, and so I was able to plan a schedule of programs that relieved the boredom of having to attend school for ten months a year and having vacation for only the remaining two months. I arranged for speakers to come in and discuss various topics, assemblies to celebrate anything from the New Moon every month to the new coat of paint our school building received every decade, and class trips to any and every place within a hundred-mile radius of the school that could be considered even remotely educational. How I managed to convince the faculty to waste so much of class time still remains a mystery, but I have a sneaking suspicion that they too were relieved to break up the monotony under which most schools labor.

We took advantage of the classes that we did have to attend. The classes that were involved in serious learning were inviolate and were treated with the proper decorum. We sat up straight, listened attentively, took neat notes, and studied fanatically in order to excel. After all, we did want to be educated.

However, the yearly curriculum always allowed for some "frill" subjects, the kind that could be easily passed without ever having to read the textbook, as long as you knew how to write intelligent essays, and class time could be spent catching up on other homework. That's when we were really in our element! We even got most of those teachers to play along with us.

I remember the time we all came dressed up as our mothers, and pretended we were attending a P.T.A. meeting instead of coming to class to learn. We affected our mothers' mannerisms, tottered about in the spike heels that were then in vogue, and interviewed our teacher on how well our "daughters" were doing in school. The teacher couldn't resist our antics and joined us in the fun, pretending to seriously answer our questions and then inviting us to have some cake and coffee, the standard fare for all such meetings.

And then there were the clubs. We had a club to match every talent. There was the glee club, the photography club, the drama club, the debating team, the good-citizenship program, the sewing club, the swim team, the band, etc. etc. etc. I opted to join the drama club and the sewing club.

It was not surprising that I joined the drama club, for by the time I was in high school, I was an accomplished actress. I'd had plenty of opportunity to perfect the art. With my parents, I often acted happy even though I was sad. With my classmates, I often acted secure and infallible, even when I was feeling especially vulnerable. Even with only myself as an audience, I played many roles.

Conceivably, it was my parents' silence that led me to

repress what I truly felt. To a large extent, they too were play-acting at life, and I followed their example. It worked for me for most of my childhood years, but with the onset of adolescence the real me yearned to break free. I wanted to know where I came from and where I was going, who I was and if I could like that person. I wanted to know if others could like me, too.

The talk with Marjorie on the day that my mother had a *yahrtzeit* made me realize that I would find life a lot easier if I could only be more open. However, I had spent so many years simulating a character other than myself, that I was hesitant to introduce a revised self to my classmates. We were used to interacting in a certain way and there was little room for change.

That's why I was so excited to hear that Marjorie was considering switching to Bais Yaakov for high school. The Hillel school had classes only through the eighth grade and Marjorie's only other option was going to the public high school. Her father was pushing for that route since it would bring his daughter a few steps closer to his goal: going to public high school was what "real Americans" did. Her mother, though, sided with Marjorie. She was too frightened of the changes that were sweeping the country in the decade of the sixties, to release her only daughter on its public playground.

Upon my urging, my parents intervened to break the stalemate at the White home. I don't know how they convinced Mr. White to agree to send Marjorie to Bais Yaakov, but in due course my good friend was registered in our school. Not only that — she insisted that she no longer be called Marjorie, but that from then on she would answer only to Miriam. The fact that Mr. White accepted that condition was even more amazing than his agreeing to send Miriam to Bais Yaakov.

When school started, I did everything I could to make

sure that Miriam would have a smooth adjustment. I wanted her to fit in comfortably with her new classmates, and I wanted her to be able to develop the close relationships with them that I had missed having with mine. If she were happy, then I would be happy, too.

Miriam was lucky that the clubs involved the whole school. Thus even the freshmen had a chance to show off their talents, and I persuaded Miriam to join the clubs that I had chosen. I was able to look out for her this way, and include her in all of the activities. Miriam quickly became part of our school, and "Marjorie" was left behind.

Once a year the drama club would put on a performance to which we invited the whole community. It was really an all-out affair and everyone came. We charged admission and it became one of the school's major annual fund-raisers. How we loved staying up late every night rehearsing, till we knew our parts better than we knew ourselves! What fun we had bellowing our lines across the large empty auditorium during practice, and munching on a supper of wilted salami sandwiches and soggy pickles! On the night of the actual performance we admired each other's costumes and reveled in the feel of greasepaint melting under the spotlights.

The sewing club's activities peaked with the drama club's, for we provided all the costumes for the play. We would go to the various fabric stores and convince the owners to donate whatever material had been lying around on their shelves gathering dust. We would then get together at a member's house, raid the kitchen, pile a stack of records on the record player, turn up the volume, and let our imaginations take over. We whipped up fantastic ball gowns, official uniforms, and sinister pirate costumes. Then, we would collect all the scraps and put together hats, handbags, and stoles. We had a great time designing and creating the apparel, and the camaraderie we developed during these sewing sessions was an added bonus.

During the rest of the school year, the sewing club met to

master such skills as knitting, crocheting, and embroidery. I loved seeing a sweater or a baby blanket materialize out of a few balls of yarn, and I felt like a most gifted painter when I took a blank canvas and etched out a beautiful scene with intricate embroidery designs.

It was probably my experiences as part of the sewing club that guided me in my choice of careers. It might not have been such a definite choice had fate not intervened, but the year and the circumstances conspired to push me along a particular path.

During our senior year, we began to seriously discuss the directions our adult lives would take. We hotly debated going for a year of study in Israel versus attending a school closer to home that would better prepare us for finding a job the following year. The Six-Day War that broke out in Israel in June 1967 solved our dilemma, as most of our parents deemed the situation in the Holy Land too unstable to allow their daughters to go there for a year of study. My friends made peace with the situation and chose to attend one of the three teaching seminaries that were considered appropriate for girls of our background. My heart was set on going to Israel, however, and my disappointment was too great to just settle for second best. I was used to getting what I wanted, and if I could not get my first choice of schooling I would rather not spend another year in school at all. My parents and friends were shocked by my decision but I could not be dissuaded.

Our home-room teacher was assigned to do senior counseling. As part of her job, she would call us in to her office separately to discuss our future plans. When she asked me, in a slightly more sophisticated version, the age-old question, "What do you want to be when you grow up?" she smugly waited for me to say that I was planning to go into teaching.

Maybe it was this smugness on her part and her pat assumption that I could easily be pigeonholed into a set pattern that finalized my decision not to become a teacher. But actually, I surprised even myself when I answered, "I am going to be an interior decorator."

She was utterly shocked, and she groped for words. "Well! Well...but most of our girls become teachers."

I claimed, as respectfully as I could, that I was not part of the "most," and that I had no intention of trying to become part of them. I explained, convincing myself as I went along, that I really loved to work with swatches of material and wallpaper, greatly enjoyed manipulating the various lines in design, and that I actually dreamed in bold technicolor. I even went so far as to claim that even from a religious standpoint she would have to agree with me. "After all, God gave me a special talent," I said. "Wouldn't He want me to use it to beautify His world?"

I became so assertive during this conversation that I had to ignore the growing suspicion that my arguments were full of holes. An inner voice was telling me to slow down and think this through. Did I really want to commit myself to dealing with fabrics when I could be dealing with the spiritual realm and teaching Jewish studies instead? But by now, my ego was too heavily involved for me to back down or to even admit that perhaps I should reconsider.

Thus my conceit triggered one of the biggest blunders of my life. I could not know it then, but this rash decision would exact a hefty price. Not that there was any problem with what I decided to do; it was true that I enjoyed these things. But it was what I decided *not* to do that I would pay for dearly. After all, all the decorating expertise in the world could not design a cure for a troubled soul, but a constant familiarity with the word of God is the best antidote for any spiritual malaise. The time for such introspection, however, would come later; and for the moment I was pleased enough with my decision to ignore both the internal and external opposition to my choice of career.

CHAPTER SIX

MY PARENTS RESIGNED themselves to my decision to become an interior decorator. They were not happy about it, but they had become so used to granting me my every wish, and they were so afraid of seeing me sulk, that they decided to accept it. However, they did take a strong stand on one issue.

College life in the sixties had become synonymous with long hair, loose morals, sit-ins, and drugs. Though my father himself had earned a doctorate in electrical engineering by attending years of night school, and realized the value of higher education, there was no way he was going to allow his daughter to be exposed to the prevailing values and environment on campuses in those days. If I wanted to become a decorator, my studies would have to take place within the safe confines of my home. This could be accomplished through taking correspondence courses which, while not quite as exciting as learning the art in a classroom setting, could still provide the necessary degree.

From past experience, I knew that when my parents actually did insist on something, I had to listen to them, and there was no room for quibbling. I set about trying to find the best correspondence school, and settled on one with particularly nice brochures. I figured that if they could catch my eye with their advertising, they might be best equipped to teach me how to catch a client's eye with my decorating skills. I was astonished at how much technical knowledge I would have to amass along with what I thought of as the "fun stuff" that I was really looking forward to learning. I was committed to what I was doing, and I attacked my new studies with a vengeance unprecedented in all my years at school.

Even before I received my degree, I was hired for some actual jobs. Word got around that I had a certain flair, and my mother's friends were willing to give me a break and take me on for some minor jobs. Very often the job consisted of redecorating a child's room, which for me was lucky indeed. I adored kids and I had no trouble relating to them and choosing patterns, carpeting, and furniture they could not help but love. And of course, I'd had the pleasure of having my own room redone about six times before I was five years old! Thus I was able to develop quite a discerning taste when it came to the best in children's-bedroom fashions.

The size of my jobs grew with my reputation as a competent decorator. I was now given entire houses and even office buildings to design as I saw fit. I loved poring over wallpaper books and examining carpet swatches. The idea of choosing a color scheme that flowed throughout a whole house, or of redoing a house to resemble one from another era greatly appealed to my creativity. My clients trusted me and I felt truly blessed to be able to work at something that for me was really more fun than work.

During this time, I maintained close contact with my school friends. We had a nice, easy relationship now, devoid of the competitiveness that somewhat marred our previous association. I had always sensed that being the leader of my class and one of its top students had evoked a certain amount of jealousy, but I had not spent too much time dwelling on the situation. Now that I was studying a field totally removed from anything my friends were studying, this subtle undercurrent of friction was absent.

They entertained me with their descriptions of their new classes and their stories about dorm life. I begged them to share with me the content of some of their more inspiring lectures. I had always taken my religious studies for granted, and I had assumed that I would continue to study on my own long after I had graduated. Somehow, though, I never was able to find the right time to sit down and delve into the holy books, and deep down I really missed the warm glow they emitted.

My friends, in turn, were fascinated with my new world. They oohed and aahed over the pictures of my model homes, and gasped when they learned how much I was earning. My world was full of glamour, while theirs was predictably conventional. We constantly discussed the contrast of our respective lives, but we all felt enriched by sharing these differences.

One topic, though, we approached with equal interest. We were now passing from adolescence into adulthood, and we had reached a stage that was both exciting and dreadful. We could not stop talking and dreaming about the one each of us was destined to marry, but at the same time we each harbored a secret fear that we would be one of the unfortunate few who would never succeed in finding a husband.

It was customary in our circles that a friend or relative would introduce a young man and woman to each other. They would meet for the first time at the girl's house, which would give her parents a chance to judge whether this man had the character and qualities needed to make their daughter happy. After an exchange of pleasantries and philosophies, the couple would leave on a date in order to become better acquainted in a more casual setting. If all went well on this first date and the couple was interested in seeing each other again, another meeting would be arranged through the party who had originally introduced them. More dates would follow until the couple could be sure they were either unsuited for each other, in which case they would agree to stop dating, or until they had developed a mutual affection and felt comfortable enough with each other to go ahead and become engaged. This practice was in direct contrast to the changing mores of the sixties, but was so successful that it has remained constant to this day, thirty years later.

Since I had so few relatives, I was worried that there would be no one to introduce me to prospective husbands. There are few things more shattering to a girl's ego than to listen to her friends discussing their dates while she tries to avoid admitting that all she does at night is wait for the phone to ring with that all-important first call. But I needn't have worried: people viewed me as an anomaly, and as such, I piqued their interest. My friends, who had all chosen to tread the same path, were viewed at first glance as almost interchangeable. They were all "good" girls who would probably make "good" wives and mothers. How was one to pick one over the other?

I was also considered a "good" girl, but I could hardly be confused with anyone else. I was definitely not part of the pack and this worked very much in my favor. My career had given me a certain amount of exposure and apparently people liked what they saw.

At this time, American Jewish life was undergoing a major metamorphosis. Until then, many of the Jews who were born in America, and even those who had come here in the forties after escaping the horrors that had occurred on European soil, lived a double life. They tried to maintain their Jewish affiliation, while at the same time they pursued the "American Dream" at least as relentlessly as did their Gentile neighbors. Their singular lack of success in this two-fold endeavor was marked by an increase in intermarriage and a decrease in the observance of even the most hallowed traditions. It was not unusual for a father who still wore traditional Jewish garb to have a son who did not even observe the Sabbath.

In the sixties, the post-war "baby boomers" came of age and began to make their presence felt. The assassination of John F. Kennedy — the vibrant symbol of hope for the younger generation — heralded an era of social upheaval. Jew and Gentile stood shoulder-to-shoulder at the forefront of the Civil Rights movement, the anti-Vietnam War protests, and the drug-crazed radical campus revolts. They were all Americans, striving together as brothers for a common cause.

Then came Israel's Six-Day War. Suddenly, young Jews had a cause all their own, with flesh-and-blood heroes and front page headlines. Israel's stunning victory, against all odds, was a catalyst for the unexpected and widespread awakening of Jewish pride, stirring the dying embers of faith in the hearts of many who had drifted far from their heritage. No longer would they live their life as Jewish Americans. It was now time to begin life anew as American Jews. The Torah, which had served as the original blueprint for the creation of the world, would now serve as the blueprint for this new transformation.

The youth, who were those most effected by the changes of the decade, were the first to forge the changes on the Jewish front. Many began to exchange courses on the college campus for courses in the yeshiva. The former concern of most young Jewish men — to prepare themselves to be able breadwinners upon marriage, to provide their families with economic security — was replaced with the concern for the spiritual security of their future families, to keep them from succumbing to the foreign influences of the country at large. Only intense Torah study could assure the success of this struggle to keep the next generation safely and securely committed to traditional, authentic Judaism.

In turn, it was now left up to the prospective wife to assume part, or even all, of the financial concerns of the family. Whereas before she could have spent her single life as a "Jewish American princess" and her married life as a "Jewish American queen," in turn pampered financially by her father and then by her husband, she would now have to give up this material security. She could still continue to reign as queen and indeed her husband was encouraged to anoint her as such, but it would be more in the spiritual realm than the worldly one.

In the context of those times of changing values, it is easy to understand why I was viewed as a good candidate for marriage. Not only did I come from a fairly affluent home, but I now had a career that almost guaranteed a more-than-adequate income. This, in combination with my other qualities, ensured I would not be overlooked. It was small wonder that anyone with a brother, a nephew, or a neighbor who could be considered at all suitable would contact my parents in the hopes of introducing the eligible young man to us. Consequently, it was not long before I was introduced to the man who would become my husband — to the disappointment of all the aspiring matchmakers who were patiently waiting for their turn to present us with yet another young man.

I have mentioned my status at this time only to make clear and understandable how great was my fall when it came, shattering me into tiny little pieces, and how it would take more than all the king's horses and all the king's men to put me back together again.

CHAPTER SEVEN

I FIRST MET Dovid Rosenberg on a Saturday night. I was immediately attracted to the sheer Americanism that he exuded. His shock of blond hair would have looked a lot more natural with a baseball cap perched atop it, than his black hat. He introduced himself in a broad midwestern accent. I invited him to have a seat at the dining-room table and offered him a slice of freshly-baked cake. My mother had baked her Austrian specialty, an apple kuchen heavily laced with cinnamon. She claimed that no suitor would be able to resist the fragrance of apples, cinnamon, and raisins — and she was right. She was positively beaming by the time Dovid had consumed three slices of the cake.

Maybe it was the hope of more of the same cake that led Dovid to arrange for a second date the following Monday afternoon. My mother spent the whole morning baking a Sacher torte, and it was while we were sharing this delicacy that we found out all about Dovid's family.

"I wish my mother baked like this," he said, "but all she has time for are the simple cakes. Don't get me wrong, though — her cakes are delicious too. When we were little, she used to stay home with us, but once we got to a certain age and could manage by ourselves when we got home from school, my father needed her to work with him in the business."

"What does your father do?" my father asked.

"He's a photographer. Have you ever heard of Simcha Studios? They're the only observant photography outfit in Chicago, and they've expanded quite a bit over the past few years as the community's grown."

"Are you planning to join the business?" my mother asked.

"Not at the moment," Dovid answered. "Actually, my older brother just started working there. He got married last year and just had his first child. He was learning in *kollel* until then, but he wanted to start working as soon as his son was born. I myself would like to learn as long as I can, before starting to work. I have a friend with four children who's still in *kollel*, and I'm hoping to have at least that many before I stop learning full time."

My father cleared his throat. "And just how are you planning to manage that?"

Dovid hesitated a moment before answering. "Well, I have some money saved up from my summer jobs over the past few years, and I figure I could do a little tutoring on the side, and then maybe if we really don't spend too much, and then maybe if my wife could work a little bit..."

"And you really think that would be enough to support a family?" my father interrupted incredulously.

Dovid looked a bit abashed, as he replied, "Yes, I...I really think it could work, provided of course that..."

My mother decided to rescue him by offering all of us another piece of cake.

Dovid eagerly accepted and came just short of giving my mother a grateful wink. This meeting was the onset of the mutual affection that was to characterize the relationship between Dovid and my mother.

It was my mother who set my father at ease regarding the financial future, and it was my mother who encouraged me to agree to see Dovid as often as could be arranged.

From that point on, our courtship proceeded at an accelerated pace. We met again on Thursday evening of that week, and then another five times in the following two weeks. Before the first month was over, Dovid and I had become officially engaged.

My friend Esther was also seriously dating during the time that I was getting to know my future husband. As a matter of fact, we became engaged to our respective fiancés only two nights apart. And not only that — both men were learning in the same yeshiva, and had even spent one semester as roommates!

We certainly had a lot in common during those months. It was quite a heady feeling for both of us, to be able to share this most exciting time with each other. We went shopping together for clothes to wear on our dates, we lent each other accessories to complement our outfits, and we even chipped in for a prohibitively expensive bottle of perfume which traveled back and forth between our two houses.

It was great fun, and we felt as if we belonged to a secret club whose door we closed to our other friends who had not yet begun to date. Of course, we weren't terribly obvious about it, but our friends must have picked up on what was happening, because before long we found ourselves totally isolated from them. We had only each other as confidantes. And that's when the trouble started. We were two people who were competitive by nature, and now we were thrown together without anyone else to diffuse our rivalry. This brought out the worst in our natures.

There is only one "best boy" in any yeshiva. To hear the talk in yeshiva circles, one may find that hard to believe — for it seems that the "best boy" becomes engaged at least once a month! But it's doubtful that the turnover rate from "merely good" to "best" is quite that high.

Every girl loves to hear that she is dating the "best boy," which explains why the superlative term is used so often. Most of the time it doesn't matter anyway: who cares enough to probe whether a particular boy is really the best, the second best, or if he is only a runner-up in third position?

We cared.

It started innocently enough. Esther hesitantly told me about her upcoming date with a young man named Shimon Goldring. She didn't want to hurt my feelings in case nothing was brewing on my end, and so she was greatly relieved when I told her that I, too, would be meeting someone for the first time at the end of the week. How delighted we were to discover that our prospective dates attended the same yeshiva, and had even attended the same high school years before.

As soon as we could, after our dates, we got together and compared notes. "How tall is he?" we asked each other. "Does he smoke? Does he have a beard? What color suit was he wearing?"

We laughed as we discovered that both Dovid and Shimon were about five feet ten inches tall, neither of them smoked, both were clean-shaven, and both of them wore a navy-blue suit. If I hadn't known better, I would have begun to suspect that we were dating the same boy!

We were even more amazed to discover that on our dates we had both ordered a 7-Up and both of the men had ordered a Coke. "Oh, this is so much fun!" we told each other excitedly as we prepared to part. We promised that we would get in touch immediately after our next date, and once again fill each other in on what had transpired.

We met at my house on Tuesday afternoon. Esther's large family was always tripping over one another in their small house, and we knew that we would not have any privacy there. After getting settled comfortably on the porch swing, we began to talk. This time we exchanged confidences on what we spoke about on our dates. We had already covered the basic details of our dates earlier, and we were eager to discuss deeper and more important points.

We realized we had both touched upon the same topics over the course of the dates. We had conversed about religion, about attending yeshiva versus attending college, and about how our backgrounds had influenced us to become what we were. It was gratifying to learn that both couples considered the same issues to be matters of concern.

We felt even closer to each other than we had earlier in the week, for not only were we actually *doing* the same thing, sharing an important stage in life, but our minds seemed to meet in a way they never had before. We were sorry when it was time to part, but we looked forward to meeting again after our next date and to further intensify our friendship.

We met again on Friday night after our mothers lit the Shabbos candles. We escaped to my room where we could be sure of not being disturbed, and settled ourselves on the soft carpet. Leaning forward eagerly in the fading light, we both asked in unison, "Well, how did it go?"

"You first!" I told Esther, laughing.

More than eager to comply, she regaled me with a description of the restaurant that she had gone to with her date, what they had ordered from the menu, and the stories they made up about the lives of the restaurant's other patrons, all of whom were strangers to them. "Your turn," she said, pausing to catch her breath. "What did you do?"

Feeling a bit bad that we had "only" gone for a walk to the park, I tossed my hair and said quickly, "Never mind that. The who, what, when and where is kind of boring anyway. Let me tell you about the insight that Dovid offered on this week's portion of the Torah." Then I proceeded to recount exactly what Dovid had said, remarking that it was a nice change of pace to listen and share in the conversation of such an erudite young man. "You know," I said, "I spend most of the day talking to clients about colors and textures and prints, and sometimes I feel as though the more intellectual part of my mind is just rotting away. Talking with Dovid is so refreshing! He's got such a keen and analytical mind that I actually feel that my brain is rejuvenating when I am with him and..."

Esther, not to be outdone, interrupted me and said, "I know exactly what you mean! Shimon is very astute and when he tells me about what he's learning, I find that I really have to concentrate if I want to follow what he's saying. He is so deep and incisive that the *Rosh Yeshiva* selected him as a study partner for the afternoon session."

"My," I said, my cheeks burning slightly, "that really is a coincidence. The *Mashgiach* just asked Dovid if he would learn with him once the new term starts."

"Really?" Esther queried a bit skeptically, and then there was silence.

Suddenly the mood in the room was not as congenial as before. We both changed our positions on the carpet at the same moment, bumping into each other as we vied for the same foot of empty space. We laughed at our clumsiness, but the atmosphere did not lighten. The tone for the evening had been set and a short while later Esther got up to leave. She politely bade my mother and me "Good Shabbos," and we did not get in touch with each other again until our respective engagements a couple of weeks later.

We had grown close enough before that time that we did not have to actually verbalize our pact of silence. We both knew that we agreed to discontinue any discussion of our fiancés' respective intellectual prowess. We smiled at each other with forgiveness in our eyes, and by the end of the second night of engagement festivities we felt we were on firm enough ground to start shopping for our trousseaux together. We arranged to meet downtown on Monday of the following week.

Our shopping excursion went well. We stocked up on linens and kitchen utensils in the morning, had lunch at a kosher restaurant in the neighborhood, and then spent the afternoon visiting print shops where we examined the newest designs in wedding invitations. We returned home as it was getting dark, exhausted but pleased with our purchases. We'd had so much fun that we scheduled another shopping trip for three days later.

The day dawned bright and clear, a perfect day for a drive. I called Esther and suggested I pick her up in my car so she could avoid the bother of getting to the shopping mall by bus. She quickly agreed, and when I pulled up in my new compact Ford, she was already waiting at the curb in front of her house.

"What a cute car!" she exclaimed as she folded herself into the passenger side.

"I'm glad you like it," I answered. "Dovid likes it too, and he's getting quite comfortable driving around in it. We figure that with a car we won't be so limited in our choice of apartments, because we can get something that's not necessarily so close to the yeshiva."

I noticed that Esther remained silent while I continued to prattle on about the car, the apartments we were considering, and the dining-room set that I'd picked out with Dovid. This was unusual for her, as Esther was generally a vivacious talker, but I attributed it to the fact that she might have been fatigued. It was not easy preparing for a wedding and preparing for classes as a first-year teacher at the same time. I silently congratulated myself on having chosen a different profession, one that did not induce such tension.

When Esther finally did begin to talk, it was on a different matter entirely. She described how Shimon had come to supper the night before and how her mother had prepared a truly festive meal. Her older brothers and their wives had joined them and all of her younger siblings, even her baby sister, were allowed to stay up until the dessert plates were cleared. There was so much noise and laughter emanating from their small house, she recounted with a happy chuckle, that one of the neighbors had knocked on the door and jokingly asked if it was actually the night of the wedding, and had the family forgotten to invite him?

I suppressed a twinge of jealousy as Esther told this story: No one would ever wonder about noise coming from our house; if anything, it was the *lack* of noise that always struck people as strange. My parents had developed an obsessive need for quiet as they grew older. My father's ulcers acted up when there was too much excitement, and my mother suffered periodically from migraine headaches. I had stopped inviting crowds of friends over once I graduated from high school, in deference to their needs, but I had never really adjusted to the new silence. For a moment, a certain painful door opened and oh, how I wished that I could be part of Esther's large and congenial family! But I instantly clamped down on the thought, for I recognized it as a betrayal of my parents who loved me so dearly.

By the time Esther finished talking, I had pulled into a parking spot right next to the entrance of one of the more exclusive department stores. We made our way through the throngs of shoppers and though Esther wanted to stop at the cosmetics counter, I insisted we take care of selecting dinnerware first.

We rode the escalator up to the third floor, where I determinatively headed for the china department. Esther seemed a bit lethargic as I looked through one pattern after another, but I again attributed her lack of interest to tiredness.

"Come on, Esther," I said as I playfully poked her in the ribs. "Which pattern are you going to choose?"

Such a look of anger suffused her face that I instinctively ducked, thinking she might hurl a whole stack of china at my head. "Stop it!" she shrieked, to the astonishment of the shoppers nearby. "Do you think that everyone can afford new cars? Do you think that everyone can afford the rent of ritzy apartments filled with the best furniture and laid out with complete sets of Lenox? Other people have more than one child that they can afford to spoil! Why don't you just grow up, or better yet, why don't you just leave me alone?"

I hung my head, stunned and fighting back rising tears. With a sob caught in my throat, I mumbled that I was sorry. I don't know which of us was more hurt. Esther turned away and I could see her back quiver with controlled crying. I gently put my arm around her shoulders and together we made our way to the ladies' room. We washed our faces, and when we were more composed we each apologized and insisted we had not meant to be hurtful. But the words had an empty ring to them. The day was ruined, and we drove home in silence.

We continued to call each other occasionally, and we attended each other's weddings. We even visited each other in our new apartments once we were married. But our relationship was just a superficial one now. We were being extra-careful not to tread on each other's toes, and this inhibition made any kind of closeness impossible.

I suffered greatly at this loss of a good friend. I lay awake some nights during my engagement, alternately berating myself for being so insensitive to someone else, and blaming Esther for hurting me in one of my most vulnerable areas, that of being an only child.

Well, I firmly resolved to never again brag about my good fortune — "Once burned, twice shy." Therefore, I will not write about my dates, my engagement, or my wedding.

"But you're an old married woman by now," one might say. "And all that happened a quarter of a century ago."

True. But still, I will never take the chance that a description of my happiness may make someone feel shortchanged. Suffice it to say that my Dovid was the best boy in the yeshiva; my dates were more exciting than anyone else's; the tenderness of my engagement period remains unmatched; and my wedding...well, what a wedding!

CHAPTER EIGHT

"MAY YOU HAVE the merit to build a true house in Israel!" Our wedding ended with these traditional words of blessing from our guests. ("A true house in Israel" means a faithful Jewish home blessed with family harmony and with children who are raised in an atmosphere of love of God and His Torah.) I graciously nodded in acknowledgement as I bade them farewell and thanked them for coming.

Sheva Berachos, the traditional seven days of celebration for the bride and groom, were under way. How thrilled we were to socialize as man and wife! We were wined and dined each evening in royal splendor and indeed, no king and queen could have received more esteem than that which was lavished upon us. Neither could any couple have experienced more fatigue than we did. But how could we have slept when there was so much to fill our time? We both had an insatiable curiosity about each other's life before we had met, and no part of that life was too small to examine and share.

We stayed up talking every night till long after our hosts for the evening had retired, to finally fall asleep when daylight started creeping into our room. We would sleep until we were awakened a few hours later by the noise made by the rest of the world's preparations for a new day. Begrudging ourselves even an hour of our day for a nap, we would continue to talk and talk throughout the day, until it was time to get ready for yet another round of celebration. By the last night of *Sheva Berachos* we were so tired we actually fell asleep just when it was time to leave! We would have missed the final party given in our honor had not one of our new neighbors chosen that night to welcome us with a freshly-baked cake. Her insistent banging on the door finally roused us from a deep sleep and we made it on time to the party with a wedding gift from the Highway Patrol: a brand-new speeding ticket!

In spite of our exhaustion, we enjoyed each one of these nights to the fullest. It was wonderful to mingle with family and friends while we ate exquisitely prepared meals and listened to muted wedding music played on the piano. We whispered to each other all evening long, keeping quiet only during the speeches that were part of the ritual of the week-long celebration. We were so tired we had trouble understanding the more esoteric references to the Torah which were invariably included in these speeches, but we immediately perked up when the speaker would praise one of us. This praise was also part of the ritual. Everyone savored the opportunity of endearing the bride and groom to each other, and of watching the bridal couple as the recipient of the praise would blush with humility and the spouse would beam with pleasure at the kind words.

Each speech would end with the refrain that had been proffered to us on our wedding night: "*She-tizku livnos bayis ne'eman b'Yisrael*— May you have the merit to build a true house in Israel!" These words would serve as our cue to resume our endless whispering and as our hostess's cue to serve the next course. Within moments of the end of the speech, the din in the room would escalate as the ladies rose to help serve, and the men made a commotion congratulating the speaker. These words were the bell that released us from the confines of sitting still and paying attention, and allowed us a brief recess to loosen up before the next speech began.

Only one person seemed impervious to the change of atmosphere at the end of each speech. I first noticed this exception when a cousin spoke at the conclusion of the meal on the second night of *Sheva Berachos*. When everyone else started to clap and smile upon hearing Dovid's cousin wish us the merit of building a true Jewish home, I happened to glance over at my mother and my heart skipped a beat at what I saw: Her hands were clenched in her lap and her face was frozen in a grimace of pain. I started to rise to make my way over to her, when she gave herself a small shake as though she were emerging from a trance. Then she looked like her normal, smiling self again. The whole scene was over so quickly that I convinced myself that nothing unusual had taken place. I enjoyed the remainder of the evening and thought nothing of what had transpired until two nights later.

That night it was my husband's friends who feted us. There were a lot of men who attended the evening's repast, but since there were only a few women, we were all seated in a small alcove in view of, but separate from, the men. I was seated directly across from my mother and so I could not help but notice her reaction to the speeches. Added to that was the fact that for the first time in our married life my husband was, for all practical purposes, out of earshot. I couldn't whisper to him so I busied myself folding the paper napkins into fans and studying the faces around me. I noted that my mother looked intrigued when words of Torah were spoken, and smiled when either of us was praised. But then, when the many speakers of the night would close with the usual refrain, my mother would almost physically distance herself from the crowd. Her eyes glazed over and her shoulders hunched forward, until she would suddenly remember where she was and then she would straighten out and rejoin us with a smile.

I don't think that other people noticed these peculiar incidents; they were too busy with the party. But I noticed them, and they frightened me. I pitied my mother. And with that pity, I am ashamed to admit, came annoyance. This was my time of jubilation, the most important time in my life. I did not want it marred by any negative emotion. My mother's strange reaction to the speeches pulled me up short and I resented this invasion of my cloudless bliss. I determined that at the first opportunity, I would get to the bottom of her disturbing behavior.

CHAPTER NINE

WE WERE INVITED to spend Shabbos at my parent's home following the week of festivities. We arrived an hour before sundown, so I had plenty of time to put on my new dress and to carefully apply my makeup. I wanted to look beautiful for my new husband, and I also needed the self-assurance that being well-groomed would give me, to confront my mother about what was bothering me.

Shortly before the sun set, my mother lit the Shabbos candles. I watched her cover her eyes as she murmured the blessing, and I noticed the tears trickle down between her fingers as she swayed gently back and forth. Then it was my turn. I, too, lit Shabbos candles now. The blessing was still unfamiliar and my eyes remained dry throughout. "Funny," I thought. "My mother doesn't understand all the Hebrew words, so why is it that she cries when she says it, while I, who have no trouble comprehending the words, cannot invest them with any emotion at all?"

When we finished reciting the blessing we turned to our husbands and wished them *Gut Shabbos*. They replied in kind, Dovid smiling shyly at me, and then they hurried off to synagogue.

Finding myself alone with my mother, I blurted out,

"Mommy, can I ask you something?"

"Sure," my mother answered, her smile open and welcoming. "Let's sit down on the couch and then we'll talk. I was concerned about how you were adjusting to married life. Of course, I trust Dovid and love him like a son, but still, the beginning can be kind of confusing. So feel free, Chanie, to ask me anything that you want to know."

"Oh, it's not about Dovid," I replied quickly. "It's not even anything about marriage."

"Oh?" my mother asked in a hesitant voice. "What is it about, then?"

"It's about the speeches."

"What speeches?"

I was getting nervous now and my hands felt clammy. "Uh, you know, the speeches that people made about us, about me and Dovid."

"They were very nice," my mother answered with a puzzled look on her face. "Some were a bit too long, perhaps, but otherwise I liked them. Is that what you wanted to talk to me about?"

"Well, no," I admitted. "It wasn't about the speeches themselves, but it was about what...what *happened* at the speeches."

"But what happened at the speeches?"

I took a somewhat shaky deep breath and said, "Mommy, why did you look so upset at the end of each speech? Why did you seem to be in such pain whenever anyone wished us the merit of building a true home in Israel? Isn't this what you, too, want for us?"

My mother's face turned an ashen gray. Her eyes looked blank. "Please, don't ask me to explain," she whispered faintly.

"But why?" I asked, shivering. There was something frightening happening in the room.

"Because some things cannot be explained."

"Everything has an explanation," I insisted.

"No, not everything. Please, Chanaleh," she begged, using the pet name that she had not used since I was a little girl. "Do not ask."

Remembering all of the unanswered questions of my childhood, I couldn't let the matter rest. I jumped up from the couch, barely able to control the urge to childishly stamp my foot in frustration. "Look at me," I said, extending my hand in front of my mother's face. "I am a married woman. I have a wedding band on my finger! I have a wig on my head. I'm no longer a child. You're not being fair to me. I need a mother who will see me as an adult. You're still treating me like a child. Why can't you be like all the other mothers who treat their grown daughters as friends?"

A look of such intense misery and pain passed over my mother's face that at that moment I detested myself for having inflicted such grief. I tried to grab my terrible words back, but they teased me by floating just out of my reach like the elusive bubbles blown into the wind by the careless flick of a child's wand.

My mother's face crumpled. "You are right. You are no longer a child..."

"Please," I interrupted, sinking back onto the couch, "you don't have to explain. Never mind, Mommy. I'm sorry that I said anything."

"No, you are right," she insisted. "You do need a mother, a mother who will treat you as an adult. I... I, too, needed a mother, but I haven't had one since I was a child..."

I sat there, a fresh young bride, looking at my mother's familiar lined face, and I couldn't imagine her either being a child or needing a mother.

"I will tell you, Chanie, what you have asked me." What had I asked for? I myself didn't know. "It was 1939," she said. "My sister was engaged to a wonderful boy...his name was Tzvi. I remember how he looked... The wedding was scheduled to take place eight weeks after the engagement, but times were tense. We knew that war was imminent. We kept hearing rumors about what was happening to the Jews in the neighboring countries that were already ravaged by the war. But we didn't believe these rumors," she said, her voice breaking. "How could such rumors be true? Would you believe such things, Chanie? But even the fact that such stories could even be fabricated filled us with fear. My family decided to wait no longer. My sister's engagement was shortened to three weeks, and it was decided that she would get married in our house, with just our family and enough men to make a *minyan*."

I nodded, feeling strangely guilty thinking of the excitement that had preceded my own wedding the week before. The guilt was an old familiar feeling: Here I was happy and careless, while *they* ...*then*... But I closed my eyes and made myself concentrate on my mother's words. "We tried to make the house look as festive as possible. My sisters and I picked all the flowers in our garden, and we wove them together to decorate the wedding canopy. We helped our sister dress in her wedding finery, and though she looked beautiful, her eyes were sad and her face was pale. Our hearts went out to her. How different this wedding day turned out to be from the one that she had dreamed about! We tried to distract her with our cheerful patter, but our father interrupted our efforts, urging us to hurry. The groom was waiting, the invited guests were tense, and a sense of foreboding seemed to permeate the house."

My mother looked around our living room suddenly, frowning in confusion. I imagined that she was trying to experience living in both houses in one moment: that other house that I pictured in grim black-and-white, and this one, our technicolor American house. "The ceremony was completed in record time, and her new husband sat at the head of the long dining-room table as we all partook of the sumptuous meal we had helped our mother to prepare. After we finished eating the soup, our oldest brother, Yitzchak, stood up and began a discourse on the weekly portion of the Torah." It's coming, I told myself. I was cold and I began to tremble. "He compared our sister Miriam's virtues to those of Miriam the Prophetess, and explained why these virtues were so essential in the founding of a Jewish home. As he turned towards the newly-wed couple and started to wish them, 'May you have the merit to build a true house...' the door was violently flung open!"

My mother buried her face in her hands and began to cry out loud. I felt as if my blood had turned to ice water. I was frozen, rooted to my place. "Go on!" I whispered.

"Four men in SS uniforms entered the house and roared with fury at the sight of the lavish feast. They kicked over the table, bellowing with rage, shouting obscenities. Then they grabbed us, one by one, threw us onto three trucks that were waiting in front of our house."

"Oh, Mommy!" I burst out, my numbness broken with a flood of tears. But she seemed stronger now, as if recounting the terrible, unthinkable story gave her strength.

"In the chaos, I became separated from the rest of my family. They were all shoved into the first two trucks, while I, desperately pleading to be with them, was dumped into the third truck. The last memory I have of my family is of my father trying to support my mother, with the help of my newly-married sister. Her bridal veil was torn and her beautiful dress was splattered and stained.

"My brother was never able to complete his blessing, Chanie. Build a home?" she cried out. "Build a home *where*? In Israel? Where is this home that she was supposed to build? What kind of home was it supposed to be? Where are the children who were supposed to fill this home? Where are the grandchildren who were supposed to visit this home?" My mother began to sob in heart-wrenching agony, while I wept with her. There were no answers to her questions.

"Why didn't he bless her instead with the wish that she should merit a true *grave* in Israel? Was her merit so small that she should not deserve even that?"

My mother collapsed into a shuddering, hunched-up ball. I wrapped my arms around her and hugged her tightly to me. My tears mingled with hers as we rocked together to and fro, drawing comfort from our closeness.

With a last gasping sob, my mother pulled herself erect. "Chanaleh, it's Shabbos," she said. "We mustn't cry on Shabbos." I saw her gazing at me with such compassion through the film of my misty eyes, but my tears continued to flow. I couldn't stop.

"Chanaleh, let's talk about happier things. Let's talk about you. You asked me what I wanted — of course I hope that you will merit the building of a true house in Israel! I pray that the house will be very large," she said, laughing a little, "and that it will contain many rooms and that you will fill those rooms with twelve children of your own. And I pray that you will live long enough to see each of those twelve children have twelve children of *their* own..." At last my tears subsided.

So immersed were we in our conversation that we did not hear the footsteps on the front porch. As the knob turned and our husbands entered, we sprang apart. My father and my husband looked at us in confusion, at our red, puffy eyes and the pile of sodden tissues lying between us that bore testimony to the intensity of our discussion. Wordlessly, they entered the kitchen to bring the wine to the table. Then they began to sing *Shalom Aleichem*, the song that welcomed the Sabbath angels who had accompanied them home from the synagogue.

The angels brought an air of peace to our Shabbos table. As my father and my husband continued to sing, my mother and I had a chance to collect ourselves. We put on brave smiles and by the time the Kiddush wine was poured, it was barely discernible that just moments before we had been in such emotional agony.

Our spirits lifted during the course of the meal. The sumptuous tastes and the delicious fragrances of the Shabbos food soothed us in a way that no words could have done. My new husband's rich baritone merged with my father's softer voice in the traditional tunes and lulled us into a state of well-being.

By the time we finished chanting the *Birkas ha-Mazon* after the meal, we all felt content, satiated, and sleepy. My parents wished us *Gut Shabbos* and retired to their room. When I started to yawn, my husband suggested that we also call it a night, and I agreed that we certainly could use the sleep. Before long we were both ready for bed, looking forward to eight blissful hours of luxurious slumber. We were relaxed and happy and we fell asleep with the good-night wishes still on our lips.

The angels had departed earlier that evening and must have been well on their way when the demons of the past entered the house. They came in their hideous black uniforms with the death-head embossed on their collars and their unsheathed swords in their hands. As they held their swords upright and aimed for the unprotected flesh, a piercing scream filled the night.

It had been years since that scream had filled the house, but on this night, long-buried memories had been unearthed.

The sound woke me and I once again burrowed deep down into the blankets as I had done when I was a child. My pigtails had long since been lopped off and my short hair was neatly tucked under my white kerchief. Only the tail of that kerchief could be seen above the covers. Still, I felt no older and no more secure than I had felt as a child. I lay there cowering and shivering, hoping that the scream was really only a part of my own nightmare, but when I heard the voices murmuring from the adjacent room I knew that it was not my own dream that had awakened me.

I was startled to hear a voice whispering my name. So enveloped was I in my cocoon of blankets and terror, that I could not absorb that there was another person in my room. It took great concentration to identify the voice of my new husband, a voice I had been listening to with such pleasure for the better part of the past two weeks.

"Chanie, what happened?" he asked gently. "Was that you who screamed? Did you have a nightmare? Would you like to talk about it or would you rather just try to go back to sleep?"

I was too befuddled to answer right away. I did wiggle my way out from under the blankets and with damp hands I gripped the covers, willing my body to stop trembling. I cautiously opened my eyes and met the concerned gaze of my husband. He looked down at me with love as he patiently waited for me to answer him.

With great effort I sat up in bed and stammered, "I...I... j-j-just c-c-can't talk about it. I...I... w-w-want to, but I just can't."

"It's okay. You don't have to tell me anything that you don't want to. Should I get you a drink of water? Will that make you feel better?"

"No, Dovid, I'll be fine. But could you do one thing for me? Could you just sing for me? Could you just very quietly sing *Shalom Aleichem* for me? Maybe your singing will bring back the angels and I won't feel quite so frightened."

My husband started to croon in a gentle voice. The sweet sound masked the murmuring in the next room. My fingers eased their grip on the covers and my head fell back on the pillow. I allowed the sound of Dovid's voice to lull me back to sleep and when I next opened my eyes, the room was bathed in sunshine. I was alone in the room, the events of the night a dull but throbbing memory.

CHAPTER TEN

IT WAS THE RESILIENCY of youth combined with the single-mindedness of the newlywed that allowed me to put the trauma of that Shabbos in the darkest recess of my mind. I opened up the bottom drawer of my consciousness, flung the incidents of that Friday night inside, and quickly slammed the drawer shut. I ignored the litter of mistaken childhood impressions and the fragments of underdeveloped notions that filled the drawer to overflowing. Yes, I did have unanswered questions and haunting concerns and I did know that if I sorted through this drawer, I might yet find some solutions to these mysteries, but I decided to save that particular chore for another day. This type of spring cleaning was suitable for a day that was clouded over by April showers, not the first sunny weeks of my married life. Now was no time for cleaning out a drawer in such an old and scarred piece of furniture. I was busy with more modern pieces.

As I mentioned before, we had purchased a dining-room set; since then, we had acquired a bedroom set as well. But we had a very makeshift dinette set: the table consisted of a slab of plywood balanced on two sawhorses. Moreover, our living room was totally bare. So now I chose to spend my time selecting new furniture. It was certainly a more enjoyable activity.

Every moment that I was able to salvage from the work that I was doing for clients, I spent decorating our own apartment. I chose all the furniture and the accessories in a contemporary style. I was so much more comfortable with the new than with the old. The old was past and buried while the new beckoned with tantalizing promise. My color scheme revolved around the blues and greens. I loved the feeling of expansiveness that the colors of sea and sky offered. Within a few short weeks, our apartment was the envy of the neighborhood.

Now we were all set to play house. I was the Mommy and Dovid was the Tatty, and as for the babies, well, they would arrive in due time. Not to worry.

We set up the rules of the game. They were, perhaps, more sophisticated than the children's version, but they did not differ by all that much. We established who would do each chore and who would assume each responsibility. But when we went grocery shopping for the first time, you could easily tell that we were still children at heart.

We each took a shopping cart and then we raced each other straight to the snack aisle. We filled our carts with potato chips, pretzels, corn chips, and candy. Then we had to rearrange the carts so that we could add the bottles of Coke and 7-Up without crushing all the bags that we had already selected. As a token to our new domesticity, at the last minute we tossed in a couple of bottles of detergent, four crunchy apples and a bag of carrots. We happily pushed our loot to the cashier and paid for it all with a newly embossed check.

When we came home we neatly packed away the detergent, the fruit, and the vegetables. The remaining groceries we set out on the table along with napkins, cups, and a bowl of ice. We settled ourselves comfortably in the dinette and munched away, drawing satisfaction from the crunchy sounds punctuated with the noise of soda being slurped through the cubes of ice. We indulged in our favorite pastime: talk, talk, and more talk. By now we were so finely attuned to each other that we would often start to say the exact same thing at exactly the same time. We would laugh whenever this happened, marveling at our closeness. Surely, no other newlyweds could be such kindred spirits!

We shared our snacks and our conversation until midnight. No one was urging us to go to bed and we reveled in the freedom of staying up as late as we chose. But with two empty one-pound bags of chips and three empty bottles of soda marking the passing of the hours, we decided it was time to call it quits. Dovid had an early-morning study partner and I had a new client to see the next day. We could not afford to sleep late and we could not afford to go without any sleep at all. Reluctantly we cleaned up and headed off to bed.

We had so much fun snacking and talking that first night that we repeated it the next night. This quickly became the highlight of our day, the time when we could look forward to sharing all that we had done or thought about since the morning.

Soon I noticed that my once-clear skin was no longer so clear, and I figured that it was all the junk food I was eating. Still, my skin had never been like this. Since I'd always had a penchant for snacks and ate as if I were allergic to anything remotely nutritious, I was surprised that I should have such a strong reaction to what was, after all, only a slight modification of my usual diet.

Then I started to feel unwell. I'd wake up in the morning with this strange queasiness which lingered throughout the day. All the food that I prepared seemed singularly untempting and even my craving for candy diminished.

One of my neighbors noticed that I looked a bit green around the gills one day, and she approached me with sympathetic solicitude. "Are you feeling okay, Chanie?"

"Not really," I replied."But I don't know what's wrong with me. I just feel all-around yucky! I can't look at food, and I'm feeling so tired."

"Congratulations," she said, smiling. "That's the way everybody feels when they're pregnant."

I can't imagine what kind of naiveté made me reply, "Who, me? Pregnant? Oh, it couldn't be, because...well, because..."

My neighbor hitched her baby more securely onto her hip, reached out and patted me on the shoulder, and offered me any assistance that she could provide.

When I was alone again, I tried to finish my stammered sentence to myself: ...Because...because I had just turned twenty; because I had just gotten married; because I had just finished decorating my apartment; because I had not gotten to know all of my neighbors; because I had not gotten used to the new schedule; because I had not gotten enough sleep! Wait. So what? What did all that have to do with whether I was pregnant or not? Hey, what do you mean? What do you mean that all of that has nothing to do with all of this? But I haven't yet had a chance to think about *this*! So, think!

I started to think, and I started to get excited. Could it really be true? Could this really be happening to me? Me? Chanie? A mother? I hugged myself in exhilaration. Then I ran to the bedroom mirror. I stood very straight and stared at myself long and hard. Then I tentatively pushed my stomach out and studied the new image in the mirror. I started to dream. In my mind's eye I grew bigger and bigger. I expanded till I was ready to pop.

The sound of a truck backfiring pulled me back to reality. Wait. I don't even know if it's really true. I haven't even told Dovid. Should I call him in yeshiva? No, it's not fair to disturb him. But I can't wait! Grow up. A little self-control is not too much to demand. Especially if you're going to be a mother. Okay, I'll wait. I'll try to eat some lunch. Oh, but

I can't! I forgot — I can't even think about food! You have to. If you're planning on being a mother, you'd better eat. Okay. Okay. Just leave me alone.

The afternoon dragged on. Twice I put my watch to my ear to check if it was still running. I just had to speak to my husband. Then the phone rang. It was Dovid! "I might be a little late tonight, Chanie. You don't mind, do you?"

"What? You're going to be late? Tonight?"

"What's the matter, Chanie? I didn't think you'd mind, so I just offered to help my friend Moshe with some packing. He's moving tomorrow. I'll probably be home before you can even miss me. Is that okay?"

"I guess so," I muttered, trying to keep the disappointment from my voice. "I'll just keep supper in the oven so that it will be warm when you come home." I hung up and restlessly began to pace the floors of the apartment.

The packing took longer than Dovid had anticipated. When he finally got home, supper was all dried out. For the first time in our married life (which was not so long), I didn't welcome him with a smile. "Where were you?" I cried. "I waited for you the whole day, and you didn't even bother to call me and tell me that you'd be so late."

"Chanie, what are you talking about? I did call you."

"You called me, but you told me that you'd be home before I even missed you. Oh, Dovid! I *did* miss you. I missed you so badly!" And as another first, I burst into tears.

My husband looked at me in confused helplessness. "But Chanie, I'm only an hour later than usual. I'm flattered that you missed me so much, but really it's nothing to get so upset about."

"Yes, it is," I sobbed. "If we're going to be parents, we're going to have to be more responsible. We can't just stay up all night, and...and come home whenever we want!"

"Chanie, what on earth do you mean? Sure, God willing, we'll be parents one day. But what does that have to do with my being late today? Has anything happened? You're not making sense?"

"Yes, I am, Dovid," I blurted out. "We're going to be parents — now!"

"Now? Today? Chanie, are you feeling well? Do you have fever?" Dovid asked me with growing concern in his voice. "Anyway, we just got married. What do you mean 'now'?"

"Dovid, I'm just trying to tell you..."

"Oh-h," he said, comprehension flooding his face. "You mean that you..."

"Uh-huh, that's exactly what I mean! Dovid, you're going to be a father. I'm going to be a mother," I said, wiping my face with a crumpled tissue.

"You're sure?"

"Well, not really. But I haven't been feeling well lately. I didn't tell you because I didn't want to alarm you. But now it does kind of make sense. And, oh Dovid, wouldn't it be great?"

"Wait, Chanie," Dovid, the realist, replied. "Isn't there some kind of test? Then we'll know for sure, and *then* we can start to get excited. Why don't I make you a cup of hot tea, and then maybe you should to go sleep early. In the morning we'll drive down to the hospital and you'll take the test."

I gave myself over to his ministrations and did exactly what he said.

Two days later the lab corroborated my neighbor's assertion. I was indeed pregnant.

As soon as we had the results, we rushed to the phone to call our parents with the wonderful news. As luck would have it, my parents' line was busy. But my in-laws answered on the first ring. "*Mazal tov*!" they exclaimed in unison as soon as our first rush of words was out. "That's really marvelous!" my mother-in-law said. "Can we tell Chaim and Bella, and Gedalia and Sara? They'll be so happy to know that their kids are going to have a new cousin!"

"Um...I'd rather you wait a couple of weeks," I replied. "I haven't even told my parents yet, and we're still trying to adjust to the news ourselves. So, if it's okay with you..."

"Sure," my mother-in-law interrupted. "Anything you say. Just take care of yourself, and don't worry about a thing."

We hung up and tried to reach my parents again. My father answered the phone. "Is Mommy there?" I asked. "Please stay on the line, though, Tatty, because there's something we'd like to tell both of you."

"Is everything okay?" he asked nervously.

"Oh, fine, fine! Please call Mommy, okay?"

When my mother picked up the phone and we announced our news, my father said softly, "That's wonderful, kids. Thank you so much for telling us." Then he added in Yiddish, "*Zol zein mit mazel* — It should be blessed with good fortune."

My mother just gulped. She didn't say a word. I wasn't insulted, or hurt, or perplexed, though. I remembered our talk that Friday night and I knew that she was simply too overcome with emotion to say a thing.

I answered her just as silently. I said to her, without uttering a word, "Here's to you, Mommy. This is the beginning. This is my first, but it's your first, as well — the first of the twelve. This one is yours as much as it's mine. It's my gift to you."

As our silent conversation traveled across the wires, I felt in total harmony with my mother. I was finally able to start to repay the person who loved me more than anyone else. I had started to hand her the gift that no one else could give her. I had great hopes that this gift would allow her to finally bury the dead. I began to wrap this gift with the hope of a new life — a new life for my mother, and a new life for me. A life without terrible dreams. A life without screams in the night.

CHAPTER ELEVEN

MY MOTHER-IN-LAW kept her word and didn't tell her other sons that I was pregnant until the two-week grace period was over. It was important that I had those two weeks, because as soon as Bella found out, she called me, shrieking hysterically.

"Wow, Chanie, I just heard the news! That's fantastic! How are you feeling?" My excited sister-in-law didn't wait for an answer and just rushed on. "What doctor are you going to? Who recommended him?"

I managed to interrupt her long enough to tell her that I didn't have a doctor yet.

"What?! You haven't gone for your first appointment? What are you waiting for? Well, maybe it's better that you haven't, really... that way you can use mine! Now, listen — I'm going to tell *you* a secret. I just found out that I'm expecting again, and we may even be due around the same time. Should I schedule an appointment for you when I make one for myself?"

"Wait a minute, Bella!" I laughed self-consciously. "Is...is your doctor good?" That wasn't what I had meant to say, but I was so overwhelmed by the fact of being pregnant that I couldn't yet imagine myself going to a doctor. That was indeed a new stage...

"Of course he is! Do you think Chaim would let me go to a doctor who wasn't good?! His office is on Michigan Avenue, and you know that only the best doctors have offices there," she explained, beginning to sound as if she were talking to a child.

"Uh...okay..." I muttered uncertainly.

"Don't worry about it, Chanie. Just let me take care of everything. I'll let you know what time the appointment is. I'm going to call right now."

Bella called back a few minutes later to inform me that we both had an appointment for the following Monday morning. We would meet at my parents' house, which was only a short drive from Michigan Avenue.

Bella picked me up from my parents' house, as we'd arranged. I thought that maybe my mother would like to come along, but Bella's efficient, breezy manner, together with my mother's — and my own — inexperience and reticence about this new situation, made us both shy. She didn't ask and I didn't suggest that she come. As I put on my seatbelt in Bella's car, I could see my mother waving from the window. For a moment I had a sudden desire to run back into the house I grew up in, throw myself into my mother's arms, and cry, "Mommy, I'm not ready to go to an obstetrician and have a baby!"

But Bella was pulling out of the driveway, and the moment passed. She put me at ease on the way over, telling me what to expect at the doctor's office. By the time I was settled in his waiting room, I was relaxed enough to start browsing through the parenting magazines. I had all but exhausted the reading material on the end table and had just started to fill out an order blank for maternity clothes when the nurse ushered me into the examining room.

I sat in the silent, empty room, waiting for the doctor to come in, for half an hour. My stomach started to twist and turn with unnamed anxiety. I counted the tiles on the floor, and then I counted the tiles on the ceiling. I counted the letters of all the words on all of the boxed supplies, and then I multiplied them by the tiles on the floor, and then I divided them by the tiles on the ceiling. Occasionally I glanced at my reflection in the mirror above the small sink. A pale, nervous young face looked back at me. I wished my mother were sitting in the waiting room outside, ready to smile at me with her anxious smile.

"Mrs. Rosenberg?" the doctor asked cheerfully. Dismissing the thought that "Mrs. Rosenberg" was my husband's mother, I managed to nod and come up with a faint "Yes." He did a quick examination, and congratulated me on my pregnancy. Then he scribbled a prescription for vitamins and iron pills, and beat a fast exit out the door.

I was officially pregnant.

Well, if further confirmation of my pregnancy were needed, we soon had it. The honeymoon was definitely over. The intelligent, creative, radiant wife with a sweet disposition that was once me was replaced by a nauseous, grumpy, worn-out hag.

The female experts (i.e., those who were already mothers) and all the medical books referred to my discomfort as "morning sickness." I began to wonder if it was called so because it was supposed to occur only in the morning, or because it started in the morning and continued till the next morning. My stomach could not tell time. I turned a permanent shade of sallow olive and the queasiness stayed with me from dawn till dusk.

My husband was confused by this metamorphosis, but the male experts (i.e., those who were already fathers) assured him that all of this travail would be over at the end of the first three months. When the female experts comforted me with the same assurance, we both relaxed and began to count off the days of the first trimester.

We greeted the second trimester with relief. Not only did

I expect to feel better, but we also knew that the time of potential miscarriage had passed. As with all parents-to-be, the specter of this possibility had loomed in the shadows of our minds, and now that I had entered the fourth month of pregnancy, we put that anxiety firmly behind us.

To celebrate, I set off on a shopping spree to buy maternity clothes, admiring the "lady-in-waiting" look in the mirror, pirouetting this way and that, and imagining myself filling out a svelte maternal design. But even during my shopping excursion my stomach continued to heave. Didn't the experts say three months of this and no more?

I guessed that I must be the exception that proved the rule. "Morning sickness" lasted all day long, and the fourth month proved no different from the second. While my neighbors in the same situation started to radiate with that special glow unique to pregnant women, I became progressively more sallow. While they began to scintillate with pre-partum energy, I became dizzy with exhaustion. Inevitably, I began to wallow in my misery and I couldn't help but ask, "Why me?" I became engrossed in feeling sorry for myself and in counting how often I vomited in one day.

Cooking, formerly a favorite pastime, became torture for me. I had to clench my fists and take a deep breath before I could even remove a chicken from the refrigerator. One look at its pale, uncooked flesh had a disastrous effect, as did cleaning it and especially smelling it simmering in the pot. Totally drained from this sequence which repeated itself every Thursday night, I tried to arrange for us to go away for Shabbos as often as we could.

We accepted any invitation that came our way, but most weekends we alternated between visiting my parents and visiting my in-laws. Both sets of parents were thrilled to have us. My parents loved seeing their new son at the table, and my in-laws loved their new daughter. When we went to their house, the Rosenbergs would often invite Dovid's brothers and their families. They would tease us about being newlyweds, and though I was sometimes too worn out for that kind of banter, it still brought a tinge of excitement to be part of a "big" family at last.

When we arrived at my parents' home one Friday afternoon, my mother greeted us with the news that Naomi, one of my former classmates, had become engaged.

"Is she having the girls over on Shabbos?" I asked.

My mother hesitated. "Yes, there's a party in the afternoon," she said. "But Chanie —"

"Oh, great! I'd love to go. I'm so glad that we came to you this Shabbos. I haven't seen my friends for such a long time, and we have so much catching up to do. This is the perfect opportunity for all of us to get together! Let me call Miriam so that we can arrange to walk over together."

"But, Chanie, it's a pretty far walk for you, in your condition," my mother said.

"Oh, it's not that far! And the walk would do me good, Mommy. Don't worry, I was just at the doctor's this week and he said everything's fine." I didn't add that he seemed concerned that I was "carrying a bit low." I didn't know what that meant so I didn't think about it. "He did say I should eat more," I went on, "but you know how rotten I've been feeling, and I can't eat a thing when I'm at home. Anyway, you know I always eat plenty on Shabbos at your house, and I'm sure that a walk would give me even more of an appetite."

My mother was silent. She was weighing her reluctance to make me unhappy, against her conviction that something was not good for me.

I rushed in with more words to block out her silence. "I take the car everywhere I go all week, and I really could use the exercise. Anyway, how would Naomi feel if she knew that I had been here for Shabbos and didn't even stop by to congratulate her?"

"You could always call her on the phone!"

"But Mommy, the Shabbos afternoons are long now and

I could use some entertainment. Don't worry — we'll have plenty of time to talk before I go. I wake up early these mornings, whether I want to or not, so while the men are in shul, we can spend some time alone together."

"Oh, Chanie, it's not that! Do you think I would stop you from meeting your friends just so that I could have the exclusive pleasure of your company? It's just..." She hesitated, and I knew she was groping for a reason to justify her feeling that I shouldn't go. "It's just that most of the girls in your class aren't even married yet, let alone pregnant. Don't you think they might feel envious seeing you like this?"

"I'm sure they would be happy for me! I'm sure that they'd find it encouraging to see that one of their classmates had moved on to the next stage in life."

My mother sighed. "I still think that it's better if you don't go."

"But why? What are you so worried about?" I asked impatiently.

"Look, Chanie, you're not a child anymore, and I can't forbid you to go. I would just feel a lot more comfortable if you stayed home. But do whatever you want."

The next afternoon, since I was feeling unusually restless and longing for some fresh air to alleviate my nausea, I decided that my mother's worries were unfounded. I explained to Dovid that my parents had always been very overprotective. The fact was, I longed for freedom from the restraints of my childhood and though I felt a bit guilty, I decided to go after all. I tried to make my mother laugh a little, telling her that I would look twice before crossing the street, I would make sure not to trip, and I would sit the whole time at the party!

I airily wished my family *Gut Shabbos* and headed out to meet Miriam and some friends at the corner, so that we could all walk over to Naomi's house together.

The party was in full swing when we got there. I rushed

over to congratulate Naomi and then I settled down in front of the punch bowl. My friends were excited to see me. They admired my human-hair wig and commented shyly on my new figure. I was used to being the center of attention, but I felt a bit bad when at one point I noticed that there were more people crowding around me than around the bride-to-be. I went over to talk to her and drew the other people with me. We passed the rest of the afternoon chatting and singing. It was so much fun to be among my good friends again that I had a hard time returning home with Dovid to our neighborhood which was a good distance away.

Two weeks later as I entered my sixth month of gestation, I found out exactly what my mother had been worried about. I was feeling a bit better and had even managed to keep down a couple of meals. For the first time in months, I felt up to cooking the Shabbos meals and so we decided to stay home and just enjoy each other's company.

For the afternoon meal, I had prepared the *cholent*. The rich bean-and-meat stew always acted as a soporific and I had barely managed to start on the dessert, when my eyes started to close. I didn't even clear the table before staggering off to bed for a long nap.

I awoke two hours later with a stomachache. "Must be the *cholent*," I thought. I had not eaten this stew for such a long time that I figured my stomach wasn't up to it yet! I tried to ignore the discomfort, but the pain only grew stronger.

Late afternoon turned into early evening. My husband had already left for shul, for the *ma'ariv* service, when the pain became intense and I realized that it might not be indigestion. I became truly alarmed, for the cramps were lower down than the typical stomachache and they were steadily becoming worse. They followed a precise rhythm, a tightening up followed by a brief respite.

I lay down on my bed, almost doubled over with pain. The moon shone in through the window, bathing the furniture in the darkened room with an eerie glow. From the street came the summer evening sounds of teenagers playing ball and I wondered if I should call out to them for help. But I lay still and did nothing, while a growing fear clutched my heart. I strained to hear my husband's footsteps returning from his prayers. *Dovid!* I cried silently. *Hurry!*

When he finally returned, we raced to the hospital, not even taking the time to call my doctor. My teeth started to chatter as my husband tore through one red light after another, honking furiously all the while. We screeched to a halt outside the emergency room, I climbed out of the car, was thrust into a wheelchair, and rushed to the obstetrics ward.

Many hours later, after a protracted labor, it was over. As I lay in the recovery room, my teeth were still chattering, but now my whole body convulsed in uncontrollable shivering as well. I begged for more and more blankets to restore some warmth to my traumatized body, but all of the blankets in the world could not dispel the cold of the grave.

CHAPTER TWELVE

I HAD ALWAYS THOUGHT of time as a long piece of rope, stretching from Creation, at the bottom of the rope, to the end of all days, at the top of the rope. Man's job involved climbing from the bottom to the top, holding on to the rope for support in his ascent from the past to the future. "Remember the days of old; consider the years of each generation."

But there is another dimension to time. On this continuum of past leading to future, time diverges from the straight path, and forms a circular track. At the beginning of every year, man purchases a ticket for the train that sets out on the year-long journey around this track. En route are many stations and the train stops at each station at exactly the same time every year.

Some stations are warm and friendly; some are exciting, and you are tempted to disembark and look around. Other stations are more somber.

And then there are the dark and dismal stations. They are full of shadows and pain. If you can help it, you remain on the train during the layover. As often as not, the electricity at these stations is out. The plumbing is outdated. The station is infested and you can hear the keening of the creatures of the night penetrating the darkness.

It was at one of these that my personal train broke down two years in a row. It was not enough that the Angel of Death waited for me there that first year and took away my hope. No, after that first time when he was given permission to strike me, he struck me yet again exactly one year later. The quivering slice of the new moon that had ushered in the Jewish month of Av feebly illuminated the tracks as the train chugged its way into the station...

It was on the eighth day of that month that he set about his task. I woke up that summer morning to the hot and stale air of an oppressive heat wave. I was famished, and I sat down to have tea and toast for breakfast. But I was still hungry. While I ate, I glanced at the Jewish calendar that was hanging on the opposite wall. As I stared at the date a wave of shock went through me. It was exactly one year ago that I had lost the baby. No wonder that I could not get full. My body demanded to be filled again with what it had once contained.

My introspection was interrupted by the jangle of the telephone. I decided not to answer its insistent ring. I did not want to talk to anyone. I did not want anyone to talk to me. I wanted to remain alone with my thoughts.

Five minutes passed, and I had sunk more deeply into my grieving, when the phone rang once again. I chose to ignore it, but it rang and rang and rang. On the fifteenth ring I picked it up.

"Hello?" I said faintly.

"May I speak to Mrs. Rosenberg?" an impersonal voice asked.

"Yes, speaking," I answered.

"Is this Mrs. Connie Rosenberg?"

"Chanie," I corrected. "Yes, it is."

"My name is Irene, Mrs. Rosenberg. Your father asked me to phone you. I'm calling from Sinai Hospital. There's been an accident. Could you come here right away?"

"A what? Who was in an accident? Let me talk to my father!"

"I'm sorry, but your father can't come to the phone right now."

"Where is he? What's this all about? Please tell me what's happened."

"I'm sorry, Mrs. Rosenberg, but I am not authorized to release any information over the phone. I suggest you come to the hospital right away. You can have me paged when you come to the front desk at the Silverman Pavilion. Ask for Irene. I'll speak to you then."

The taxi took forever, it seemed. I flew through the door of the Silverman Pavilion and came to a halt at the front desk.

"May I help you?" the receptionist asked with a smile.

"I'm supposed to speak to someone, Irene somebody."

"Would you like to have a seat while I page her for you?"

"No...thanks...this is an emergency. Could you please page her as quickly as possible?"

"Irene Millstein," the intercom crackled. "Irene Millstein, please report to the front desk. Irene Millstein..."

A middle-aged woman, her hair drawn back in a bun, came hurrying towards me with a purposeful stride and said, "Mrs. Rosenberg? Please come to my office." She beckoned me to follow as she made her way over to one of the cubicles at the end of the hallway.

"Oh, please!" I cried, hurrying to catch up to her. "Can't you please just tell me what happened?"

"Just one moment," she said, closing the door behind her. "Maybe you should sit down."

Reluctantly, I sat down on the edge of the chair that she had indicated.

"Well," she said, "as I told you on the phone, there's been an accident. A driver going south on Route 22 apparently lost control of the wheel and crashed head-on into the car that your mother was riding in. He was killed instantly and your mother..." Her tone became very gentle. "Well, your mother has been critically injured." I gasped. Her words floated around me in the air, refusing to sink in.

"Critically injured?" I echoed. Each syllable sounded disconnected. I willed myself to concentrate on what she was saying.

"She sustained a severe concussion, her spleen has been punctured, and all of her ribs on the left side are cracked. The doctors are trying to stabilize her so that they can operate. There is a great deal of internal bleeding and her blood pressure is dangerously low."

What was this blankness I was feeling, this strange calm? Only my voice trembled. "Can I see her? Is she conscious?"

"She's conscious, but she is in a great deal of pain. Your father is with her now."

We rode the elevator together to the ninth floor, and she guided me over to the intensive care unit.

Irene motioned to my father through the glass windows. He caught sight of us and came toward me, his face a mask of sorrow. We nodded wordlessly to each other as he exited and I entered the room.

I made my way over to where my mother lay, hooked up to every conceivable machine. She was surrounded by so much technology, that at first I could barely discern her frail form lying on the bed. When I drew closer, her eyes fluttered open and she whispered, "Oh, Chanaleh! I'm so glad that you came in time. I wanted to see you just once more."

"Mommy!" I cried. My strange numbness was replaced by a rush of intense love for her. "You'll see me many more times. The doctors are going to operate. You'll be fine, Mommy, don't worry, everything will be okay."

"No, Chanaleh. My time has come. I just want to tell you, you have always made me so very happy. You are the best daughter a mother could have. Please Chanaleh, just continue to make me proud of you. Take care of Tatty. Take care of Dovid. Remember all that we taught you. Remember who your grandparents were. Remember how they died while sanctifying God's name. I'll be watching over you." She closed her eyes again, her energy spent.

"Mommy!" I cried again, collapsing over her still form. "You can't leave me yet! You gave me everything, and I haven't been able to repay you yet. You know that I tried, Mommy." Now I was weeping like a baby. "I wanted so badly to make you happy, I tried to give you a child..."

"Chanie," my mother interrupted in a strangled whisper, "you will still give me a child. Come a little closer. I cannot talk anymore. Just one thing. You will still give me a child...maybe even two...maybe even twelve...I'll be watching over you...I'll be praying for you..."

Mommy, don't go! I'm not ready yet. Mommy, please, Mommy!

The EKG machine traced a flat line. The paper spooled silently to the floor.

CHAPTER THIRTEEN

THE SEVEN DAYS of mourning began on the eve of *Tishah b'Av*, the ninth day of the month of Av, the saddest day of the year for the Jewish nation. My tears provided the salt for the egg which is traditionally eaten at the mourning repast. I tried to compartmentalize my feelings of loss, but the collective loss of my nation at the destruction of the Temple and the personal loss of my mother ran together in the river of my tears. Loss and destruction took on a new clarity.

The days of intense mourning, the *shivah*, passed in a fog. People came in and out, many of them bringing food that we were too upset to eat. The only presence I remember clearly was Miriam's. She was there with us, keeping the house in order and escorting people in and out. I sat with my father, both of us numb with grief, being comforted by all who knew us. We heard endless stories of my mother's selflessness during her youth, her years in the concentration camp, and her years as a wife and mother. I was able to fill in a little more of the background in the tapestry that depicted the person whom I had loved more than anyone in the world.

The weeks after *shivah* plunged me into depression.

Whereas during the week of mourning I was distracted by all the company who came to comfort us, the period afterwards was marked by a sense of isolation and too much empty time in which to think. My thoughts vacillated between the agony of losing my own mother and the frustrated hope of becoming a mother myself.

It is known that God allows time to heal a mourner's despair, and as the months passed, the intensity of my grief for my mother did begin to subside. This left me with a crystallized focus on my childlessness. The fact that I had become pregnant so soon after my marriage led me to believe that it would be only a short while until I would become pregnant again. As the months passed, I realized that I was mistaken.

The months turned into years, and the years were tumultuous ones. Their emotional twists and turns all revolved around the central fact of my life: my infertility. My hopes soared, and then they plunged. Again and again. They expanded at the merest hint of a new treatment, and they shrank with despair as yet another treatment failed.

I went to all kinds of doctors. I went to the biggest specialists. My portfolio grew. I set up appointments with professors at prestigious medical schools, arriving at their offices armed with a briefcase of medical history. I made appointments with the entrepreneurs of the latest in nutritional quackery, and then canceled them. Placebos and panaceas were not what I needed.

I forced myself to check out yet another doctor, to withstand yet another course of treatment, to take another battery of tests. These tests were not fun and I could not approach them with a carefree attitude. Nor did I receive the same high marks on them that I used to expect whenever I took a test in school.

After being painfully examined by the doctor, bled by the lab, and X-rayed by the department of radiology, I would meet with the latest specialist in his consulting room. He would greet me with a solemn expression and then proceed to discuss the results of the test. "Well, Mrs. Rosenberg," he would say in a very deliberate tone, "I have both good news and bad news for you. The good news is... and the bad news is... so I would suggest we approach it this way... Now, we've had some very good results with this treatment and I certainly hope that it will work for you. Of course, we've experienced failure, too, but that's to be expected. And as for the side effects of this treatment, you may find this or that discomfort. On the other hand, we will have to monitor you strictly for some of the more dangerous complications..."

Months and years, years full of months. My visits to the doctors continued. Their faces varied, their tests varied, and their treatments varied. But their lack of success remained constant.

Motherhood began to take on the guise of fantasy. I had a recurring dream in which I was holding a baby in my arms. How I loved that dream baby! Then I would wake up, my face soaked with tears as I struggled to consciousness and realized that in real life my arms were still empty.

How can I describe what I felt throughout those long years? My emotions were so overwhelming that even now as I try to record them, I have to force my pen to write what my memory is so reluctant to reveal.

How to explain the pain I felt as my body deceived me? I had always taken pride in my femininity. I had loved to adorn myself with pretty dresses, experiment with the latest in makeup, and set my hair in the most flattering styles. Now my very femininity was threatened. Barrenness was its antithesis and in my barren state I felt crude and ugly. From grade school onwards, we were all coached in the role of the Jewish mother. We dwelled on the powers and contributions of the Matriarchs and were trained to follow in their footsteps. I had joyfully begun to follow in the path that they had forged, but then I found myself stranded on a bridge whose far side was suspended in midair.

What a toll my barrenness took on my family! I had always had a deep and satisfying relationship with my father, and I longed to comfort him after my mother's passing. But what did I have to offer him? He was already in his seventies, and conversation about the past inevitably caused him to break down and cry. I couldn't bear to watch my father cry. But as for conversation about the future...what future? So we talked about the mundane. We discussed his work, and his car, and his schedule, but we shelved all of the important topics. My father remained uncomforted. And I — I had not only failed my mother, but now I was failing my father as well.

My in-laws tried to comfort me. They constantly invited us for the weekend and they were always generous in their praise of my appearance and of my talents. But I had begun to view myself as a failure and as such I could only perceive their hospitality and compliments as empty gestures and words. After all, I had failed them as well.

At some point I convinced my husband that we should stay home for the holidays rather than go to family. "After all," I rationalized, "why should I bring my misery to someone else's holiday table?"

"If that's what you prefer, it's fine with me, Chanie," Dovid said gently. My husband always tried to please me, but I could tell that he felt very lonely at our empty table.

As time passed, spending one holiday after another with only each other as company wore us both down. The empty places around the table seemed more and more desolate. I finally decided that we needed a change, and happily I hit upon an idea. Thinking that my oldest brother-in-law would surely understand the reason for my request, I called him and said, "Listen, Gedalia, I was just talking to Dovid and we both felt it would be really nice if either your Shmuel or Joey would come out to us for the Sukkos holiday. Either one is old enough to help Dovid build the *sukkah* and decorate it, and then he could stay for the first two days and get acquainted with yeshiva life. It would really be an experience for him, and..."

There was silence for a moment. "Well, Chanie, thank you but... it's okay if they visit you for a couple of days during vacation time, but for the holidays? I'm surprised that you'd ask. A son's place is at his father's table. I wouldn't think of letting either of the boys go. I hope you're not angry with me, but I'm sure you understand."

Sure I understood! Tears sprang to my eyes and my cheeks burned as I replaced the receiver. I understood that my brother-in-law did not care enough about me to understand my needs. I was humiliated. I would never ask a favor from him again. Let him keep his precious sons, I fumed. It probably wouldn't have worked out well, anyway.

And so we pulled away from family more and more. We even found it an effort to go to family celebrations. We keenly felt the passing of time with each family wedding, bar mitzvah, and bris. It was a toss-up whether we suffered more from the pity of our relatives or from the curiosity of strangers. At each celebration I was inevitably seated next to someone who would start a conversation with the question, "How long are you married?", followed by the next question: "And how many children do you have?" My answer would ensure an embarrassed silence for the rest of the meal, and the evening would be ruined.

My relationship with Dovid became charged with unanswered questions. How did he feel when he watched his friends learning with their young sons? How did he feel when all of his friends danced with their children perched upon their shoulders on Simchas Torah, and he danced all alone? Did he blame me? Did he resent me? Was he sorry he'd married me? And, above all, did he still love me?

As we walked home together from shul on the last day of the Pesach that preceded our fifth wedding anniversary, I watched the families strolling along beside us. The mothers proudly pushed the baby carriages, while the fathers tried to keep the rest of the kids together as they pranced about in the sunshine. What a pretty picture the children made as they skipped along in their matching outfits!

One little boy in particular caught my attention. He was wearing blue velvet pants and a ruffled white shirt. His golden hair was long and curly and his lashes fringed the most mischievous pair of eyes that I had ever seen. He darted in and out between his brothers and sisters while he sang a Pesach song in a lilting voice. How lucky his parents were to have him at their table!

I stole a glance at my husband to see if he was as aware of the people around us as I was. No, he seemed totally absorbed in recounting to me the gist of a lecture the dean of the yeshiva had recently given. But could he really be that oblivious? Surely he noticed the contrast between our twosome and all the other families. He was surely trying to protect me, and I, in turn wanted to protect him.

A thought came unbidden into my mind. Yes! I recognized it. It grabbed hold of me during the meal as I served and cleared the table. As I lay down for an afternoon nap, it hung on tenaciously and would not let me sleep. It nagged and nagged at me and by nightfall it had forced me into a decision.

"Dovid," I announced firmly after he returned from shul, "there's something that I want to talk to you about."

"Sure, Chanie. We can talk about it while we clean up and put away the Pesach dishes."

"No, Dovid. The cleaning up can wait. This is important, and I want us to sit down."

"Okay, what's up," my husband said amiably, pulling out a chair. "Talk!"

I forced myself to look steadily into Dovid's clear eyes, and I took a deep breath. "I want a divorce."

He stared at me incredulously. "What did you say?"

"I want a divorce," I repeated.

"Chanie! What have I done to make you say such a thing?" he demanded.

"It's not you. It's me. I haven't given you a child. It's not fair to you. You don't deserve to be stuck with me. You deserve to be a father."

Dovid turned pale. "How can you even talk like that, Chanie? How can you even let such words pass your lips?"

"I'm serious, Dovid. This is the way I feel. Please don't be angry at me."

"But I *am* angry! This is not the way to talk. What gives you the right to challenge the will of God? What gives you the right to manipulate our destiny? Chanie, you're my wife. Our marriage was made in Heaven, and what's in store for you is in store for me."

The lump in my throat didn't allow me to reply. Dovid rolled up his sleeves, determined to begin the night's work packing away the Pesach dishes. The subject was closed.

CHAPTER FOURTEEN

AS I SLOWLY LOOSENED the ties that bound me to my family, I turned to my friends for solace. But except for Miriam, the only one who was not yet married, they were all busy with their young children. Only I — the first in my class to get married — still had no children.

At least I still had Miriam during those first tumultuous years of my grief. And she was the only one with whom I could be totally myself. I didn't have to pretend to be in a good mood if I really wasn't, and I didn't have to present the perfect veneer that I cultivated for the rest of the world. After all, we were as close as sisters, and family members love each other for the good and for the bad.

Miriam had come to lean on me more and more as the years went by. Her parents had not given up their drive to be quintessential Americans, and Miriam felt steadily more uncomfortable in her own home. Her dress and manner were decidedly Jewish and her ideals reflected all that our school had taught. The chasm between Miriam and her parents broadened, and consequently she turned to me for solace and advice.

Miriam spent at least one weekend a month with us. We would reminisce about our childhood, and about how lucky we were to have each other as confidantes. We would probe the question of how our parents' respective backgrounds had influenced our personalities as adults, and we would wonder if what they had gone through had permanently affected us.

Though the past occupied a lot of our conversations, Miriam came to us because of her concern for the future. She wanted to marry a man similar to my husband in values and outlook, and she hoped that we would be able to help her in her search. Her parents, of course, were dead set against such a match. The friction in her home drove her away to ours and she looked to us to execute the role that her parents could not fill.

Dovid and I became very involved in the match-making. We were either busy setting her up with eligible young men or busy investigating the character and abilities of the candidates other people had suggested. Our long-distance phone bills ran into hundreds of dollars, but we didn't mind. Nor did we mind the late hours we had to keep as we helped Miriam work out her problems.

Our excitement was great when Miriam became engaged to Aaron Fine, a man whom Dovid had introduced to her. Miriam was glowing with happiness and her rapture reflected back to me. It helped to pull me out of my grief and I joyously threw myself into helping my friend get ready for her wedding. I shopped with her for clothes and set up appointments for her with the wig stylist. I held her hand through the ups and downs that every bride experiences during her engagement, and I tried to prepare her as well as I could for the special challenges that marriage offers.

I had invested so much energy into the whole affair that by the time Miriam got married, I was sure that no mother could be more emotionally involved in the marriage of her own child. Short of actually walking Miriam down the aisle to the wedding canopy, Dovid and I had assumed the parental role. The only time I stopped crying during the whole ceremony was when Dovid was called up to chant one of the blessings that are bestowed upon the bride and groom. This was quite an honor for someone who was married only five years, and I realized that it was one way in which Miriam was able to express her appreciation to us.

I made a *Sheva Berachos* celebration for Miriam the night after her wedding. It was an elaborate affair and I spent days in the kitchen preparing special delicacies. I loved every minute of it. What better way to spend my time than to combine my creative talents with my desire to make Miriam happy?

When the first speech of the evening ended with the traditional blessings for the marriage, it occurred to me that there was a strong possibility that Miriam would bear a child before I would. I asked myself how I would feel, and I decided that my primary emotion would be joy for Miriam. I knew that I would feel a pang at my own childlessness, but I felt so connected to Miriam that whatever would make her happy would make me happy too. By the time the evening ended, I had fervently begun to hope that Miriam would be a mother before the year ended.

I tried to keep my distance from Miriam during the first month of her marriage. I remembered from my own newlywed days how I had tuned out the rest of the world so that I could spend the time exclusively with Dovid. I was sure that Miriam, too, would need this time to be alone with her new husband. I worried about her, and several times a day I was tempted to call her to make sure that she was fine, but I chose to forgo my need to know, for what I was sure was her greater need for privacy. What surprised me, and hurt me, though, was that Miriam didn't call me even once during that first month.

I still had not heard from her when I bumped into her at the supermarket about six weeks after her wedding. "Miriam!" I cried happily, hurrying over to her. I gave her a big hug. "How are you doing?" I asked, stepping away from her to get a better look.

She stepped even further away from me as she said quietly, "I'm okay."

"So how are the newlyweds? How's Aaron?"

"He's okay, too."

I was taken aback at her reticence. Miriam had always been an effusive talker, and it wasn't like her to be so quiet. Trying to draw her out, I said, "Why don't we go out for some pizza after we've finished shopping?"

"Maybe another time." Miriam looked away.

Now I was really confused. "Why not today?" I pushed. "Do you have other plans?"

"No, not really," she answered. "Okay, I guess we can go," she said reluctantly. "Should we meet at the exit in fifteen minutes?"

"Sounds good to me," I agreed, troubled by her manner. I went to finish my shopping, but I was so upset by Miriam's attitude that I forgot to get half the things I needed.

When we sat down in the bright interior of the pizza shop, I noticed that Miriam looked a bit peaked. She barely responded to my attempts at conversation and only nibbled at her slice of pizza.

"Are you feeling okay?" I asked with concern.

"I'm fine," she replied, "but I think that I'd better get going. Aaron is going to be home for lunch soon and I don't want to miss him."

I drove home from the pizza shop trying to make some sense out of Miriam's behavior, telling myself not to feel hurt, that there must be some explanation. Then it hit me. Miriam is pregnant! She may not even know. That would explain it. She probably isn't feeling well, and doesn't realize herself that she's being irritable and moody. I know what she needs! I told myself. I'll invite them for Shabbos. She surely must not feel like cooking.

That night, I called Miriam at her apartment for the first time. Aaron answered the phone.

"Hi, Aaron, this is Chanie Rosenberg. May I please speak to Miriam?"

"She's in bed already," Aaron answered. "May I take a message?"

It was only nine o'clock! Hearing that Miriam had gone to bed so early confirmed my suspicion. "No," I said. "I'll try to reach her in the morning."

When I tried to call in the morning, I kept getting a busy signal. I dialed every fifteen minutes, but I couldn't get through. Aha! I thought. The phone is off the hook. She must be resting.

I finally reached Miriam in the afternoon. "Hi, it's me. How are you doing?"

"Fine," she replied unenthusiastically.

"We wanted to invite you and Aaron to come to us this Shabbos. Would you like that?" I asked brightly.

"Thanks, but we're going to my in-laws for Shabbos."

"How about next week, then?"

"Oh, I think we're going to *my* parents next week."

"Well, what about the week after that?" I persisted.

"I'm not sure," Miriam answered. "Why don't I let you know when we have an available Shabbos..."

Was this really happening? Was my best friend giving me the classic brush-off: *Don't call us; we'll call you?*

"Okay, Miriam," I answered coldly, "if that's the way you want it!" I hung up, fully expecting Miriam to call me back immediately and apologize.

I stayed home for the rest of the afternoon waiting for the phone to ring. I waited in vain. Miriam did not call that day, nor did she call the rest of the week.

On Sunday I asked Dovid if he could try to look up Aaron in yeshiva. I thought that maybe Dovid could find out from Aaron why Miriam was acting so peculiarly.

Dovid did speak to Aaron, but their conversation was not very enlightening. Aaron explained to Dovid that Miriam simply needed her privacy, and suggested that maybe it would be better if I didn't bother her.

"*Bother* her?" I cried. "I didn't even speak to her for six weeks!"

I was genuinely puzzled. Could I have offended her in any way? I thought and thought, but couldn't come up with anything that would explain her behavior.

I didn't see or hear from Miriam for a few months, until we met at a wedding one evening. Miriam was wearing maternity clothes. I forced myself to go over and greet her, and her response was cordial but distant.

We were seated at the same table, and I waited till she sat down so that I could grab the chair next to her. I kept trying to lead the conversation in a personal direction, but somehow she managed to avoid saying anything of consequence. By the time the second course arrived, she had turned away from me completely, and she spent the rest of the evening chatting with the woman who was sitting on her other side.

When we went to check out our coats, I made one last attempt. "Miriam!" I said quietly but urgently, trying to corner her. "I know something is wrong. Maybe it's something I did and maybe not. I'm really suffering and the hardest part of it is that I don't even know why. Miriam, won't you please tell me what's bothering you?"

"No, Chanie. I'm not ready to talk yet. Yes, something *is* wrong, but I myself don't know exactly what it is. Oh, there's Aaron waiting for me. I'd better go." She hurried off, leaving me standing alone among the coats.

I came back from the wedding extremely upset. "How can Miriam treat me this way?" I asked Dovid. "What have I done to her, that I deserve this?"

Dovid had no answers. He commiserated with me, and I think he too felt hurt.

I couldn't sleep that night. Was it that Miriam was expecting and that I was obviously having problems becoming pregnant, that made her so uncomfortable and aloof? But was that my fault? I began to sink into self-pity. I needed her sympathy, not her rejection. My loss was double — not only was I childless, but I had lost my best friend as well.

All that week I had trouble sleeping, and my loneliness and need for friendship seemed overwhelming in the quiet, undistracted night. I would lie awake and conduct imaginary conversations with Miriam. "How can I possibly make amends if I don't even know where my guilt lies? How can we ever be friends again if you cast me away from you without a hearing? Oh, Miriam, won't you please talk to me?"

On another night, I tossed and turned until the hands of the clock on my night table pointed to three. I was giddy from lack of sleep, and I imagined myself saying to Miriam, "Listen, Miriam, I just saw the most fantastic ad. There's a sheep farm in Australia whose owners went bankrupt! The property is being sold at one quarter of its value. I thought you and Aaron might like to buy it! Just think — wouldn't you love to live in Australia? There's so much unspoiled nature there, and I bet you'd love the kangaroos and the koala bears. And can't you see your husband running a farm? Drinking milk fresh from the cow, enjoying the exertion of good, physical labor? Come on, Miriam, let me help you pack." As the fantasy continued to play on, I finally fell asleep.

The days lengthened into weeks and I still didn't hear from Miriam. I became numb to the pain and denied my feelings. I convinced myself that her friendship meant nothing to me, that I could do without her. I thought about her less and less with each passing day, burying my hurt deep inside me where I could barely feel it. That's why, when I got a call from her one morning, it took me a moment to even recognize her voice.

"Chanie," she said, "we get a *Mazal Tov*. We have a baby boy."

"Oh, *Mazal Tov*," I said, trying to inject some enthusiasm

into my voice. "How nice!"

"Um, Chanie, we were wondering...would you and Dovid be *kvaters* at the bris next Tuesday?"

I didn't know what to answer. I thanked her for asking us and I told her that I would discuss it with Dovid when he came home for lunch.

The rest of the morning I tried to decide what to do. Of course we had been given the honor of being *kvaters* before, at other bris celebrations, carrying the baby into the room where the circumcision took place. It was said to be a great *segulah* — a good omen — for bearing children, and we wanted to take advantage of every *segulah* that came our way. But this time was different. Not only would I be facing the usual hardship of being in the limelight and having everyone pitying me because they would know that I didn't have children, but I would also be wondering the whole time what Miriam was feeling. Was she still angry with me? Was she also pitying me? I felt that I would prefer her anger to her pity, but I knew that there was no way I could discuss either emotion with her.

Then I remembered something I had learned from *Pirkei Avos*. It had made a deep impression on me at the time and I was happy to be able to recall it now. I had memorized it in its original Aramaic — *L'fum tza'ara agra* — and now I translated it to myself: "In proportion to the pain is the gain," i.e., the more we strive and suffer for something, the more merit we receive for the experience. To be *kvater* at Miriam's baby's circumcision would bring my suffering to a new height — would that help me to have a baby?

I didn't even wait for Dovid to come home — I was afraid that I would lose my nerve and change my mind in the meantime. I quickly called Miriam back and told her that we would be delighted to accept.

Being *kvater* at that circumcision ceremony was at least as hard as I had anticipated. We went to pick up the baby at Miriam's apartment. It was the first time that I had ever set foot inside, but I didn't have time to look around because Miriam came out immediately and handed me the baby. I pasted a smile on my face and wished her *Mazal Tov* once again, and then I carried the baby out to the car.

In the car I folded back the blanket that was covering the baby's face. I had envisioned this baby's arrival on the second night of his parents' marriage. I had been so sure then that this baby would bring joy not only to Miriam and Aaron but to me and Dovid as well. A lot had transpired since that night.

How did the baby look? He seemed to be of average size. He was wearing a white knit outfit and a white bonnet. His face had the scrunched-up look of most newborns. He had cute little fingers and toes, I guess. What response did he evoke in me? None. None whatsoever. And then I thought about his mother. What response did she evoke? His mother...let's see...what was her name again?

CHAPTER FIFTEEN

I HAD VIEWED the abrupt termination of my dream to have a child, and the death of my mother, as losses which were ordained in Heaven. I believed in the Master Plan and I had been taught since early childhood that whatever God does is for the best. That message was imparted to me not only in school, but at home as well. My parents had experienced the greatest devastation in Jewish history and they had both suffered in a way that was too great for me to grasp. Yet, they never lost their faith in God. Their unquestioning acceptance of tragedy and their joy in worshiping God despite their sorrow had been woven into the fiber of my very existence. And so — at least on an intellectual level — I was able to come to terms with my misfortunes.

The loss of Miriam's friendship fell into a different category. It was not a tragedy, per se, and because of that I did not have the tools to come to grips with it. I refused to acknowledge even to myself how painful her betrayal was. I just knew that I had lost something very important, and that my life had changed.

I had always been available for Miriam; she was younger, and had always relied on me to help her solve her problems. She became the recipient of all that was good in me: she filled my need to give, a need which had grown with the passing years of childlessness. She was also *my* confidante. Whenever something troubled me, I knew that I could discuss it with Miriam. She rarely offered advice, but we had become so attuned to each other that simply by speaking with her, I was often able to work out whatever was bothering me.

Now all that had changed. I was left with a void that I did not know how to fill. This pain brought other changes, imperceptible at first, into my life. I, who had always been very disciplined, began to daydream and to delay doing the things that had always lent structure to my life. It took me longer to get dressed in the morning. I postponed writing thank-you letters. I frequently canceled appointments with clients. And I began to eat. I often found myself cramming a candy bar into my mouth or one piece of gum after another. I became short-tempered, and my moodiness surprised people who knew me. Mundane affairs began to seem like major problems to me.

Once we were invited to a bar mitzvah celebration. My husband had always been friendly with an older crowd, and a lot of his friends now had older kids. Dovid was eagerly looking forward to the event, hoping to meet some old friends that he hadn't seen in years. I didn't want to disappoint him by telling him that I would rather stay home. I had begun to brood about the event, thinking about how awkward I'd feel, how I wouldn't know anyone.

When we arrived at the hall, I picked up my place card. I was seated at Table 10 in the women's section. I was one of the first there and I waited impatiently for the table to fill up. True to my prediction, by the time everyone was seated, I realized that I did not know anyone. The women were all very friendly and pleasant. They introduced themselves, and it turned out that they were all friends of the bar mitzvah boy's mother. They looked interested when I explained that my husband was an old friend of the bar mitzvah boy's father.

Before long, though, they became caught up in their own conversation. Everyone else at the table knew one another and they forgot all about me. I didn't blame them, and I reminded myself that when I got together with my friends, I was no different. I tried to follow the conversation, but since it centered around the names of people I didn't know, I soon got confused and gave up.

Inevitably the talk turned toward their children. Now I had no trouble following what was being said.

"How do you like Deena's teacher? Isn't she wonderful? My daughter had her last year."

I was so worried that they would ask me about *my* children, that all my senses were on the alert. I busied myself with my food so that I would seem to be occupied, and then they would hopefully ignore me. It worked. By the time they exhausted the topic of teachers, I had finished eating two rolls and had started on the hors d'oevres tray.

"Where does your son get picked up in the morning?" the talk continued.

"Oh, he doesn't take the bus. We only live four blocks from school, so he walks."

"You let him walk all alone at his age?"

I finished the hors d'oevres. I leaned over to pull the vegetable bowl closer to me.

"You know, they've started to serve hot lunches at the high school. It's such a nice change from sandwiches."

"Yes, but my daughter refuses to eat them! She's afraid that she's going to get fat."

"*Your* daughter? You've got to be kidding! She couldn't be more than a size six. Now *my* daughter really has a weight problem..."

The only thing left in the bowl were black olives. I don't like olives, and I never know what to do with the pits anyway. But one of the women had started to look my way, so I pretended to be absorbed in eating again. I took an olive and chewed with great concentration. Afterwards, I dropped the pit in my evening bag.

The conversation had switched over to little children. Now all the danger signs were up and the alarm bells ringing. The women were comparing notes on disposable diapers versus cloth ones. Their voices grew louder as the proponents for each type wanted to convince the others. I ate and ate — chicken, more chicken, potatoes, while I waited tensely, my chest tight, for the question to come. But it didn't.

The main course had been cleared. There was nothing within my reach for me to eat. I was not hungry but I didn't know what to do with myself.

"Excuse me," I said across the table. Everyone fell silent. They had forgotten that I was there. Now they wanted to hear what I had to say.

"Could you please pass the bread?" I asked in a small voice. Someone pushed the bread basket my way and the conversation resumed. I had finished five slices of bread by the time dessert was served. The waiters rolled a Viennese table into the center of the room heaped with luscious confections. I stayed seated while the rest of the women at my table got up to help themselves. I couldn't eat another thing, but I was thrilled that this course marked the end of the evening.

On the way home, Dovid couldn't stop talking about what a wonderful time he'd had. "It was so good seeing everyone again! Even my old camp counselor was there, Chanie. Did I ever tell you about him? He reminded me of all the mischief I'd done. I had forgotten most of those pranks. The bar mitzvah boy spoke beautifully, didn't he? His father told me that he'd practiced with him for ages. It really showed! And Chanie, weren't the desserts fantastic? I had the mousse tart, a chocolate éclair, and one of those frozen fruits. What did you have?"

"I didn't have any dessert," I answered.

"You didn't? Why not? That's usually your favorite part of any meal. Oh, I get it, Chanie! You're probably on a diet. That's really great, Chanie. I'm proud of you. You have gained weight lately."

That was the last thing I needed to hear. I felt let down by everything and everyone. I turned to Dovid and said, "No, I'm not on a diet, and what's more I have no intention of going on one. I had a miserable time, and I didn't even notice the bar mitzvah boy. I didn't know anyone there and all I did was eat. By the time dessert was served I was too full and now all I want to do is go home and go to sleep. It's late and I wish we had gone home hours ago. Next time you can go alone, and I'll stay home."

Dovid was clearly surprised at my outburst. When I saw the hurt in his eyes, I regretted that I had spoiled his evening. But I was too upset to apologize. The evening had simply underscored for me my alienation from the rest of society. Everyone was involved with their children. Everyone except me. I was tired and tense. All I wanted to do was go to bed and forget about the rest of the world.

A night's sleep did nothing to restore my good humor. I remained cranky and irritable. It was at this time that people started to bombard me with the word that I would come to resent more than any other.

First it was Dovid. One night, after he had endured a week of my uninterrupted moodiness, he said "Chanie, I know that you've been unhappy lately. I don't blame you. But maybe you should just try to relax."

Then it was one of my clients. I had spent the afternoon with her, reviewing the plans to redecorate the first floor of her house. We couldn't seem to agree on anything. When she suggested a floral print, I told her that only a geometric pattern would do. When she insisted on white, I insisted on black. We had worked together before, but we hadn't encountered this problem at all. Finally she suggested, "Why don't we take a break and have a cup of coffee? Maybe then you'll feel more relaxed and we'll be able to sketch out some designs we agree on." I was annoyed that she had placed all the blame on me.

My friends seemed to jump on the bandwagon. Every conversation I had with one of them suddenly included a tip on how to relax. One friend suggested that I go swimming with her twice a week. Another one tried to sign me up for yoga classes. A third told me about a Jewish meditation course that was being offered at the adult education center.

Relax. Relax. Relax. All their words came together like the insistent buzzing of a fly. I tried hard to swat at this annoying creature but he lodged himself in my ear. I jumped up and down hoping to shake him loose. I slapped my hand against my head hoping to frighten him, but to no avail. He just became more firmly embedded and insisted even more vehemently, *Relax, relax, relax, relax...*

The clincher came when we celebrated our fifth wedding anniversary. My in-laws had invited us over for dinner along with my brothers-in-law, sisters-in-law, and all their kids. My sisters-in-law had helped to prepare the dinner and the food was delicious. I became involved in playing with my nieces and nephews, and for the first time in months I was talking and laughing as though I didn't have a care in the world.

Then my mother-in-law ruined it all. As someone started to cut the cake, she whipped out an envelope and handed it to me across the table. "Here, Chanie," she said, smiling. "This is a little present from us. It will help you to relax."

The smile on my face froze. I resisted the temptation to put my hands childishly behind my back. I took the envelope from her, fully expecting it to contain a prescription for a potent tranquilizer.

"Come on, open it," my mother-in-law urged. I was embarrassed to open the envelope in front of the whole family, but with everyone coaxing me to, I had no choice. I ripped it open and pulled out two round-trip tickets to the Bahamas.

"Oh, wow!" I exclaimed. "What a lovely surprise! Thank you so much!"

"I knew you would like it," my mother-in-law smiled. "You could use a little vacation and what better place to relax in the winter than a tropical island! Do you think that you'll be ready to leave in a week?"

I looked questioningly at Dovid. He turned to his mother and said, "We'll have to discuss it when we get home. I'm not sure yet about our schedule, but thanks, Mom, for such a thoughtful gift. We really do appreciate it."

When were were alone, I asked Dovid what he meant when he said that he wasn't sure about the schedule. He reminded me that it was in the middle of his winter term at the yeshiva and he wasn't sure that it was right to just pick up and leave his study partner and their intense learning, for five days in the sun. He told me that he would have to discuss it with the dean.

I don't know what Dovid said to the dean or what the dean said to him. Dovid must have told him that the situation at home was kind of rocky, or maybe he said that his wife was depressed. Whatever it was, when he came home from yeshiva, he told me that we could start packing.

We left for the Bahamas the following Saturday night, and we arrived at our condominium in the early morning hours. It was too early to start the day and it was too late to go back to sleep. We dozed off for an hour or so and then we decided to do some touring. We stumbled along with our travelers' guidebook, going from place to place, too tired to absorb very much of what we were seeing except for the bright blue sea and the strong sunlight. We were glad to call it a night by the time the sun went down.

Dovid woke up the next morning with fever and a sore throat, something that always happened to him when he missed a night's sleep. He spent the day in bed and I spent the day with a book, lying in the tropical sun. "What a great way to start a vacation!" I grumbled in self-pity. "This place costs two hundred dollars a day, and here I am all alone with a book I could just as well have read at home."

"*Relax, relax*!" buzzed the fly who had kept quiet for the previous few days.

By the afternoon Dovid was feeling much better. He was ready to join me, and suggested that we go boating. But now it was my turn to stay in the room: my skin had turned a fiery red and I was in agony. Dovid took out a boat by himself, and I sat immersed in a tub of cool water.

I was awake all night, trying to find a cool place on the sheets — as soon as I found a comfortable spot, it turned hot. The next morning my face and arms were full of blisters. We spent the day waiting at a clinic for a doctor to treat me. I had second-degree burns. I was used to waiting in doctors' offices at home, but I certainly had not counted on doing this on my vacation.

"*Relax*," the fly buzzed. "If you want to get pregnant, you have to *relax*. Don't get so aggravated. It's only a sunburn. Just *relax*."

"It may be only a sunburn," I retorted, "but it's also the third day of our five-day vacation. How can I relax if everything keeps getting fouled up?"

The doctor who treated me was short and squat and very foreign-looking. He prescribed creams and medication and admonished me for my carelessness, making comments about stupid Americans. I wondered if I could trust him with my care, but he must have known what he was doing. I woke up the next morning feeling much better. Dovid was feeling fine too.

We had a lovely time the last two days of our vacation, and I realized how much we had needed this chance to unwind together without any external pressures. I was able to face the world again.

CHAPTER SIXTEEN

I RETURNED FROM OUR VACATION determined to put the loss of Miriam's friendship behind me. Perhaps she had been my best friend, but by no means was she my only friend. I had other friends, a small nucleus of people who truly cared about me. They did so much for me that not only do I want to relate their deeds so that I will remember to be eternally grateful to them, but I would also like to keep their selflessness in the forefront of my memory to serve as a guide in my relationship with others.

If I had to isolate the one quality that they all shared and that I appreciated the most, it would have to be their ability to treat me as a person in my own right. To them, I was Chanie, first. The fact that I did not have children was only secondary. I did not feel when I was in their company that I was wearing a placard around my neck with the words "childless" blazing in neon lights. They shared their ideas with me, visited me frequently, and even discussed their kids with me.

That is not to say that they ignored my childlessness. On the contrary. They were always there for me when I was depressed and needed someone to talk to. Even when they knew that I was hurting too much to absorb what they had to say, they still hung in there just to share my pain.

When they knew that I would be receptive, they offered their advice. They would save medical clippings for me and ask me if I would be interested in hearing what they said. They would give me the names of rabbis whose blessings had helped other childless couples, and they would discuss with me other spiritual approaches that were known to be helpful. Never did they discuss my condition with anyone else. Never did they force their opinions and knowledge upon me, with one exception. There was one time when a friend strongly felt that my doctor was giving me the wrong advice. She apologized for intervening, but begged me to get a second opinion. Her insistence saved my life, and for that I can never repay her.

But I don't want it to sound as if I ran a twenty-four hour news network to share with my friends the state of my infertility. I am a very private person, and it was only my great need that led me to say anything at all. The only person that I spoke to absolutely freely was my husband. But the pain that I did share with my friends helped to preserve my sanity and cemented the relationships that I hope to enjoy for many years to come.

My friends, loyal though they were, had very busy lives of their own. They were limited by bed-time, nap-time, homework-time, and supper-time. I was not exactly sure what these times involved, but I knew that they were sacred and that I could not interfere with them. During those times, when I felt lonely, I was left to my own devices. I enjoyed a good book and a good piece of cake, and my favorite form of relaxation was to settle down with both on the recliner in my living room and tune out everything but the fiction that I was reading.

I had always viewed my apartment as a refuge from a world that did not always synchronize with me. Its cool colors soothed me and I had chosen the furniture with an eye to comfort. As my key would turn in the latch of the front door, I would feel the cares of the day fall away.

One hot August day I'd had an unusually trying time at work. After an adrenaline-pumping drive back home through summer roads packed with kids playing ball and dodging in and out between the cars, a strange thing happened. I entered my apartment eagerly, but instead of experiencing its soothing welcome, I felt an uneasy tension.

I walked into the living room, trying to draw comfort from its smooth order and good taste, from the things I had so lovingly chosen, and that meant so much to me. There on the coffee table was my ceramic vase filled with exotic silk flowers. I had purchased the vase six years ago and it did not have one single chip. The vivid flowers were free of dust and stood erect and proud. In the corner was my rubber plant, its smooth, gleaming leaves a rich dark green. I had gotten it from my mother's friends upon my engagement and it had grown to a height of six feet. The windows had cloth shades and light lacy curtains. They were as white as the day that I had hung them, and enhanced the wallpaper that remained free of a single hand print.

I walked into the dining room. I had always thought that table pads were tacky, and so my table displayed its fine wood grain. It did not have a scratch or a stain. No glasses of water had been spilled on it, and no toy had been scraped across its perfect finish. The chairs that were arranged around it were upholstered in a plush fabric, unprotected by plastic. There was only one tiny stain on all of the six chairs. My eyes wandered over to the breakfront. It still contained twelve of everything: twelve pieces of stemware, twelve place-settings of china, and twelve crystal goblets.

How much pride and pleasure I had taken in furnishing those two rooms. Now they seemed to close in on me, to threaten and mock me: "You took so much pleasure in our immaculate appearance! Don't you see that a few smudges and stains would have made us feel lived-in?"

My heart pounding, I ran out of the apartment and

slammed the door behind me. Calm down! I told myself. Go and sit outside for a while.

I walked down the stairs to the courtyard, where a group of mothers sat on lawn chairs watching their small children busily at play. The women were in the middle of an animated discussion when I appeared, but when they noticed me they fell silent.

In the silence, the words of one little red-haired girl drifted over my way. "You be the Tatty and I'll be the Mommy and Leah will be the baby."

So simple, I thought bitterly.

The mother of the redhead must have seen something in the expression on my face, for she suddenly snapped at her daughter, "Esty, why are you playing that silly game again? Why don't you play school? You haven't played that in a long time. Who's going to be the teacher?"

I felt my face burning. Did she hope to spare me with her tactless intervention? Did she think that I wouldn't recognize her ploy? But what else could she have done? Should she just have kept quiet? I might still have been hurt then, but I would have been saved from her obvious pity.

The sun began to set, and I shivered in the late summer chill. I got up to leave, excusing myself with the claim that I had to catch up on some of my decorating work.

I reentered the apartment that had ejected me a short while before. Not wanting my excuse to be a lie, I drew out the briefcase containing my current decorating project. I spread out my graph paper, my ruler, the swatches of fabric, and the samples of wallpaper. I stared at them long and hard, hoping that they would come together in my mind and help me to create a beautiful room. But they just lay there, inanimate objects with no intrinsic value.

For the first time ever, I experienced a reluctance to play around with the tools of my trade. The swatches were itchy to the touch and the colors were totally flat. "What am I doing this for?" I questioned. "Is this what my life is all about, the adornment of edifices made of wood and stone? What a superficial interest! Is this to be my contribution to humanity, the decoration of the material world?"

I was shocked at my revolutionary thoughts. "What is with me today?" I asked myself. "How did it happen that on the very same day both my comfortable apartment and my secure career turn on me? Are they both so fickle that they can change from friend to foe without any warning at all?"

I put the kettle up to boil and prepared myself a cup of tea. I pondered these new questions as I sipped the hot liquid. My thoughts darted from here to there and back again. I questioned my future, while at the same time I tried to guess what it was in my past that had led me to my present state of turmoil.

I did not realize how far back in time my thoughts had traveled until I consciously recalled a conversation that had taken place so many years before.

"Most of our girls become teachers," my teacher had maintained. How sure I was of myself when I had answered her that I was not part of the "most."

No, I certainly was not part of the "most." I was not part of them then, and I was certainly not part of them now. But now, things had changed. I was not sure of anything other than my lack of fulfillment.

"Perhaps," I thought for the first time in all those years, "I should have chosen another field. Would I not have been happier in the realm of the spiritual, teaching and passing on to others what I had learned? Would not my involvement with the metaphysical have given me something tangible to hold on to, whereas my work with the physical gave me nothing of substance to grasp?"

CHAPTER SEVENTEEN

I DID NOT REALIZE that years and years of intense emotions cannot be suppressed forever in one small beating heart. Even the strongest of hearts can be assaulted with too much pain, and break under the strain.

Since my mother's passing, it became my custom to trek out to the cemetery on the eve of the Ninth of Av, her *yahrtzeit*, the anniversary of her death. It was also another anniversary, one I did not officially commemorate but whose memory never left me. One year the summer sun beat down so ferociously and the heat was so oppressive that I had trouble prying my tongue loose from the roof of my mouth to utter the customary prayers and traditional greeting. "*Shalom lach, immi morasi.* Peace be unto you, my mother, my teacher," I began, gasping from the pain of the encounter, and feeling faint from the heat. "Mommy, where are you?" I cried, as I leafed through the pages of the *siddur* to find the special prayer that is said when one desires children. "*B'Gan Eden tehei menuchasech* — In the Garden of Eden you will find your resting place.

"Mommy, you left this world with such a pure soul. Surely, you are close enough to the One Who hears all, to intervene on my behalf!" And my tears fell then, saturating the parched earth at my feet. I began to tremble with such fierce agony that I felt my heart would crack.

I took a few steps backwards, unable to endure anymore this encounter that had left me shattered. I traveled home in silence, took out the book of *Kinos* for Tishah b'Av, changed into a pair of cloth shoes, as is customary on this day of mourning, and sat down alone with my husband to once again eat the meal before the fast, the traditional hard-boiled egg dipped in ashes.

Feeling emotionally depleted, the ashes sticking in my throat, I arose and went with my husband to the synagogue. The candles flickered in the dim light as we listened to the mournful reading of *Eichah*, the Book of Lamentations, and I watched the shadows on the wall perform their macabre dance. I saw in their shapes an image of bodiless souls holding hands for support, as the story of their murder and the destruction of Jerusalem was chanted.

I came home before Dovid and waited alone till he walked in. We then settled ourselves awkwardly on the floor, and opened the Book of Job. We spent the next hour discussing pain and human suffering and its purpose. I had trouble understanding some of the verses, but I had no trouble identifying with the subject. We sat up a while longer, talking about the *churban*, the destruction of the Temple, and we went off to bed.

I could not sleep. Was it because I was uncomfortable without the pillow I had given up for that night as a symbol of my nation's mourning? Was it because of the heavy conversation we'd had before retiring? Or was it due to the strain of the day's activities?

Well, what did it matter what the reason was? Once I realized that sleep was going to elude me, I wearily got out of bed and headed out to the balcony. I lay down on the couch there and gazed up at the starless summer sky.

The sultry night surrounded me, and my mind began to wander. It left my body behind and traveled to another land and another time. My mind's eye viewed a crumpled black-and-white photograph: There was a father with a long beard, a mother with a bonnet tied securely under her chin, twelve modestly dressed children, and even a baby in the arms of one of the children.

"Where are all these people?" I whispered into the summer night. "Where have they all gone?" I had only touched one of them, but I intimately knew the remaining thirteen. How could I not? They were blood of my blood and flesh of my flesh. "Where are they?" I demanded, my voice becoming shrill as I repeated the question.

And the night, this particular night, answered: *Chalalayich lo nikboru.* Your corpses have not been buried." The image of my grandparents, my uncles, my aunts, and my tiny cousin faded out in the night. "Where have they gone?" I heard myself cry. And I saw in my mind's eye a small pile of ashes, the only physical testimony to people who had lived in the ways of God.

"God, can it be?" As the pain in my heart deepened, I rose up and cried. "Can all of these people, standing so meekly side-by-side in this photograph, have lived for You and have died for You, and not have left a single trace in this world? I am the only remnant. You have taken all the others to be close to You...In *Gan Eden* they found their resting place. Can You leave me here alone in my barren, childless state? Can it be? Oh, God, can it be?"

And as I gazed up into the deep summer sky, the night began to fade, and the faint dawn creeping up over the horizon brought me the answer in a whisper so low that only I could hear:

"*No, it cannot be.*"

CHAPTER EIGHTEEN

AFTER YEARS OF GOING from one specialist to another, and trying treatment after treatment, I reached the point where, even if I had not quite exhausted the conventional routes of treatment, they had exhausted me. I knew it was time to look farther afield.

One of my friends encouraged me to take a more comprehensive view of my situation. "Doctors have only as much knowledge as God allows them to have," she constantly reminded me. "They can cite statistics and precise percentages to support their theories, their choices of treatment, and their prognoses. But there are other things that they don't know anything at all about." She collected stories of cases where doctors had given up hope of a woman ever conceiving, and yet she eventually had children. "There are other keys to motherhood," she claimed. "Don't leave any of them untried."

My husband strongly abided by this approach and we set off to pursue this more esoteric route. We traveled from the famous rabbis to the deans of the great yeshivas, spending many nights sitting on hard benches in their reception rooms, waiting for their advice and blessings.

I left each of these sessions spiritually uplifted, so much

in contrast to my tedious visits to doctors. I must emphasize, though, that I felt then and I still do now, that those medical visits were an essential part of our effort to pursue our goal through natural means. All of the great rabbis fully encouraged us in this approach.

I became so enthusiastic with my new course of action that I felt I was ready for an even bolder move: I decided to travel to Israel by myself and spend forty consecutive days praying at the *Kosel*, the Western Wall. This surviving remnant of our Holy Temple has been the site of our people's prayers and petitions for countless generations. It is said that praying there for forty days in a row allows a person's prayers direct access to God's Holy Throne. We planned that my husband would meet me towards the end of the forty days, and then we would just take some time off for touring and enjoying our vacation.

I contacted relatives and acquaintances in Israel, made all my travel plans, packed my bags, and boarded the plane. It was a new experience for me to travel alone over such a long distance, and I felt lonely and nervous. Despite all this, though, as the plane began to descend and the deep blue Mediterranean came into view, I was filled with excitement. And when I alighted from the plane into the bright Israeli sunshine, I felt joy, gratitude, and hope. My anxiety evaporated altogether.

For the next few days I went to the *Kosel* as early as possible in the morning, afraid of the unexpected causing a break in my count of forty days. And although I was completely wrapped up in the reason I had come to pray there, my singlemindedness could not keep me from experiencing the radiance of the Jerusalem light, the clarity of the air, and the warmth and comfort of the *Kosel*'s ancient stones.

After having successfully completed a week's worth of excursions, I began to feel unwell. Although I tried to ignore it, something did not feel right. I went to an Israeli clinic and took a pregnancy test. It was positive. Instead of being joyous, however, I panicked. We women must be blessed with very sensitive radar, capable of picking up the slightest indication of trouble.

I checked into the hospital and phoned Dovid. "Don't worry!" he pleaded with me. "I'll be there on the next plane."

I had been hospitalized in America several times, so I should have been thrilled to be in a hospital where I was surrounded by other Jewish patients; where getting kosher food was a matter of standard routine and not complicated special requests; where Shabbos candles were brought to my bedside table for me to light, and there was a synagogue on the premises for my husband to attend. But I couldn't spare a single thought for any of these things.

This pregnancy followed the course of the previous one.

Depression, though, did not set in so intensely in this holy land. My husband concluded the forty days of prayer at the *Kosel* on the eve of Rosh Hashana, the Jewish New Year. What better time to have a renewal of hope? And what better location for that renewal to take place than the Land of Israel, where every ray of light and every stone tells of renewal. Where towns and villages have grown on barren mountainsides, and fields and orchards flourish in the arid desert. Where a nation has risen again out of the ashes of the Holocaust.

Yes, being in Eretz Yisrael renewed our faith and our hope and our patience. We now turned to our new and old acquaintances for advice on how to take advantage of the new year in this very old land. They were more than pleased to inform us of any means or method whose aid was legendary in the process of being granted a child. Some of what they suggested rang true. Some did not. Dovid and I were faced with the dilemma of how to distinguish between Faith and folly.

CHAPTER NINETEEN

BEFORE MY HUSBAND had left the States, a friend handed him a piece of paper as he was leaving for the airport. "Look up this person when you get to Israel. He may be able to help you to acquire what you want most of all. May God grant you success, and may we hear good news upon your return."

One evening after I was released from the hospital, Dovid said to me, "Come on — it's time to go look for Rabbi B." With the scrap of paper on which the rabbi's name and address were written, we set out into the moonless night and wended our way through the narrow streets and twisting alleys of the Me'ah She'arim neighborhood. The howling of stray cats accompanied us. It took us a while to find the house, but when we finally knocked on the door we were warmly welcomed into a small but immaculate apartment.

The rabbi's wife invited me to join her in having a cup of tea, while my husband went in to talk to the rabbi. I was too nervous to drink more than a few sips of the hot brew, and I practically jumped out of my chair when the door to the adjoining room opened and Dovid came out. I thanked my hostess for the tea, and nervously bade her farewell.

"Tell me, Dovid! What did the rabbi say?" I inquired as

soon as we were out of earshot.

Dovid looked down at me and smiled. He suddenly seemed very vulnerable in the glow of the street light. "Before I tell you what he said, Chanie, I have to tell you something else first, something beautiful. When I told him that we've been married for seven years and that we don't have any children yet, he almost cried." Dovid paused, seeing the sudden rush of emotion his words had caused me. "You know, a lot of people really feel for us, but this was the first time I've seen someone react as though he were feeling our pain as strongly as if it were his own.

"I got all choked up myself and I had trouble talking, but he understood anyway, and he told me that there's an old man who always prays in his shul. This man's prayers have helped a lot of people, he said, and he strongly urged us to pray along with him during the High Holy Days. He then blessed us that our prayers should be answered. What do you think, Chanie? Should we give it a try?"

"Of course we should!" I exclaimed. After all, we had devoted this trip to the quest for a child. What better way than through prayer?

We didn't tell anyone where we were going, as we trudged the long distance from our rented apartment, in a more modern quarter of Jerusalem, to the old neighborhood of Me'ah She'arim. By leaving our area early and returning late, we managed to be at the synagogue for every prayer service.

I joined the women praying in their section. I didn't know any of them, and while they all welcomed me with warm smiles and wishes for a good year, I was not tempted to indulge in idle conversation. They were dressed in the traditional holiday garb of Eretz Yisrael, that had been passed down from their mothers and grandmothers; white dresses and white kerchiefs. The sky was a deep, still blue, framed by the small arched window on the stone wall beside me. I prayed with a singlemindedness that I rarely achieved at home, in more familiar surroundings. The only thought that interfered at all with my prayers that year was my curiosity about the old man that Dovid was speaking to.

When the shofar was blown to signify the end of Yom Kippur, both Dovid and I were on a spiritual high. Although we had been fasting for more than 24 hours, in the intense, dry heat of Yom Kippur in Jerusalem, we were infused with energy and walked back to our apartment like a bride and groom leaving the wedding ceremony.

After the High Holy Days, many people took the time to talk to us and advise us. Some suggested special chapters of Psalms to say at the Western Wall. Some recommended that we should be especially stringent in following certain commandments. Others suggested special formulas to drink, while still others advised us to seek the help of Kabbalists.

We became very confused at this deluge of suggestions. We didn't know what to do — was all of what we heard part of our Faith, or did some fall into the category of folly? We had no answers, so we decided to consult with someone wiser than us. We made an appointment to visit the dean of one of the great yeshivas and when we questioned him as to what route to choose, he advised us to follow the traditions of both of our families. Of course we should pray as often as we could. And of course we should follow all of the commandments of the Torah to the best of our ability. But we should be cautious in becoming involved in Kabbalistic rituals, for it was not part of our tradition to do so and there was the danger of doing things incorrectly. That would be folly.

Two days before we were scheduled to leave the country, friends of ours insisted that we include one more thing in our itinerary: a visit to the Galilee, to the holy city of Tzefat (Safed), high in the mountains. Tzefat and the adjacent city of Meron contain the graves of many great and holy men. We would do well to pray at these sites, they said. But what was perhaps just as important, was that in Tzefat there resided a wise sage of indeterminate years. His counsel was known to have helped numerous people and they urged us not to miss the opportunity of meeting with him before we went back to America.

We saw no reason not to follow their suggestion. We had planned to do a bit of touring anyway on our last day in Israel, but we knew that we would not enjoy a frivolous trip if it was in place of one more endeavor to bring us closer to having a child. We set out early in the morning, but it wasn't till late in the afternoon that we gained an audience with the elderly rabbi.

One of his disciples ushered us into the *Rav*'s study. He bade us to be seated and then he asked us how he could be of help. My husband answered that we had come to him to ask for his blessing that we would merit having a child. He explained that our dream to build "a true house in Israel" was as yet unfulfilled.

To my surprise, the rabbi suddenly turned to me and asked, "Do you do good deeds?"

I was caught off guard, and hesitated before replying, "Yes, I do. I do well in my job, and I tithe more than the required ten per cent." I was uncomfortable with my answer. It sounded as if I were boasting.

"No, that's not what I meant," the rabbi replied gently. "I'm not referring to the giving of charity, although that is very good, too. I'm asking you if you actually *do* any good deeds."

"Well," I said hesitantly, desperately searching around in my mind, "I do help to set up for charity functions. People always call on me to help them with the finishing touches for any communal affair that takes place." Why did I sound as if I were bragging again? I became even more uncomfortable.

"Do you do any good deeds that involve children?" the rabbi continued to question me.

"Well, I help in the drive to collect clothes to send over to Israel. A lot of the clothes that we collect are for poor children."

"A most admirable project," he agreed. "But what I would suggest that you do, aside from continuing with your present projects, is to get more directly involved in helping people with their children. When you see that a mother is having a difficult time managing to take care of her children, take that opportunity to help. In the merit of helping others with their children, may God bless you with children of your own. Please, let us hear good news from you."

In the clear mountain air of the holy city of Tzefat, his words resounded as indisputable truth. I knew that this was what I had come to Israel to hear. But I wondered if I had the courage and the strength to lay myself open to the pain of caring for someone else's child. I felt that I did not have to make the decision of how to carry out his advice until a later time.

We prepared to leave Israel, and in the meanwhile I put his words on the back burner of my mind, leaving them there to simmer until a time that I would feel more ready to pursue this angle. That was folly.

CHAPTER TWENTY

I RETURNED HOME GRATIFIED, and filled with new hope. I had been greatly inspired by our visits to the two spiritual leaders in Israel. Much to our loss, they are not alive today to help others except through their prayers, but we were fortunate to benefit from their wisdom and their insights. The spirituality that I had gained in the Holy Land forged new thought patterns.

But though my thoughts were changing, my habits were harder to break. I still sounded the same; I still looked the same; and I spent my days in much the same way I had spent them before our trip. I was just not ready to translate thought into action. Why? I'm not quite sure, except that perhaps it had to do with the fear of being disappointed. If I changed everything about myself, if I became "really, really good," and then if I did not, God forbid, have a child right away, how would I be able to bear it? What other recourse would I have? So instead, I became only "a little bit good," leaving myself the option of trying harder in the future.

It was a childish approach. Who was I playing games with, anyway? Was I trying to trick my husband or my friends? Was I waiting for some nameless somebody to come along and beg me, "Oh, Chanie, you know that you can do better — just try a little bit harder"? I was fooling only myself, and as is usually the case when a person is the object of his own deceit, my half-baked scheme of partial self-improvement backfired.

One day, I got home from work in the middle of the afternoon. I heard Dovid puttering around in the kitchen and I called above the din of clattering dishes as I headed to the bedroom. "I'm home, Dovid! I'm just going to change. I've got an awful headache and my feet are killing me! I'll be right there." I kicked off my shoes, threw down my wig, and stepped out of my suit. I hastily buttoned my housecoat, tied a kerchief around my head, and stuffed my feet into a fuzzy pair of mules.

"Phew, Dovid, it's awfully hot in here! Why didn't you turn on the air conditioner? Did you eat? Sorry that it was leftovers again, but I just wasn't in the mood for cooking this morning. You know, you're not going to believe what my client said to me today. You'd think that someone her age would know how to be a little more tactful..."

"Uh, Chanie, sorry to interrupt you, but I really must get back to yeshiva. I don't want to be late. We're in the middle of a complicated discourse and I want to get cracking."

Usually I was really pleased with Dovid's diligence. The one thing that I prided myself on in my marriage was my constant encouragement of his learning and my non-interference in the hours that the yeshiva had set aside for formal study. But this time Dovid had interrupted me just as I was about to tell him about the latest tactless remark someone had made to me, and I did not appreciate being cut off in mid-sentence.

"Wait a minute, Dovid — it's only five to three. The afternoon session doesn't start till four o'clock. What's your rush?"

"Oh, I just feel like going a bit early today."

"A bit early? You're going a full hour early! And since we're talking about it, Dovid, I've noticed that you've been going to yeshiva earlier and earlier since we came back from Israel. Why, sometimes it seems that almost as soon as I walk in the door, you walk out!" Trying to keep the shrillness from my voice, I lowered my tone. "Listen, Dovid, you know that I realize how important your learning is, but don't you think that we should have *some* time together?"

Dovid seemed to be concentrating very hard as he cleared his dishes from the table. "Yeah, you're probably right. We'll talk about it tonight. Okay?" He didn't meet my eyes.

"No, it's *not* okay! I want to talk about it right now. It's only three o'clock and you have plenty of time."

"Chanie, leave it alone. I need some time to think about what I want to say. Let me go now, and tonight we'll take the phone off the hook and we'll have plenty of time to talk."

But something was driving me. And the heat in the kitchen was oppressive. "I don't *want* to stay home and stew about this all afternoon, Dovid. You obviously have something on your mind, and I can't imagine what it is. You're upset with me, or what I've done, or haven't done, that's made you act like this. But whatever it is, I don't think it's fair that you should just go to yeshiva and leave me home to worry. I'm willing to listen, and I think that you should be willing to talk."

Dovid sighed. He still didn't meet my eyes. "Okay, Chanie. I'll tell you what's on my mind, but on one condition. Agreed?"

"What's the condition?" I asked shakily. Oh, how could Dovid be talking to me like this? My anger was turning into hurt and self-pity.

"You have to listen without interrupting. Then when I'm finished, I'm going to yeshiva. I don't want you to answer me right away. I want you to think over what I said and then when I come back for supper tonight, we'll do what I suggested. We'll take the phone off the hook and we'll have the whole evening to talk undisturbed."

I apprehensively nodded my agreement. "Okay, Dovid. I guess I have no choice." I took a deep breath and tried to sound breezy. "So what's my big crime?"

"There is no crime, Chanie — don't be silly. It's not a matter of something that you did or didn't do."

"So what's the matter?" I cried.

"Please, Chanie. You agreed not to interrupt. Let me see if I can explain it to you. You know that I'm not very good with words. You're the articulate one in this family, but I'll try my best."

Dovid began to pace back and forth across the kitchen. He always did this when he was agitated. Then he nervously cleared his throat, and he began.

"When we first started getting to know each other, I was so impressed by your *simchas chayim*, and at how quickly people gravitated towards you. You took such joy in everything. You always had a sunny disposition and you were so self-assured and poised that I thought that nothing could ever strike you down. Then slowly, when things did not go exactly as we had anticipated, you sort of, well, started to change. Your joyousness seemed to fade. We stopped visiting our families, and you always needed to be prodded to go to any social event. When people came to see us, you acted polite but distant. It was almost as if you were doing them a favor by entertaining them. I love people, and I had always envisioned our home as one that would attract anyone and everyone by its warm hospitality. But over the past seven years, Chanie, I can count on the fingers of one hand how often we've had company at your suggestion."

Oh, it was all true! I couldn't meet his eyes. I sat stiffly just letting his words go in, each one striking me with a blow that only the truth can inflict.

Dovid paused to collect his thoughts, and I let his words sink in. I wanted to refute them, but the truth was undeniable. He drew a deep breath and continued. "Aside from your close friends, you don't seem to enjoy anyone's company at all anymore. I remember when you used to come home all charged up because so-and-so was so friendly, and so-and-so was so talented." He smiled sadly. "You'd rave about almost anyone that you chanced to meet, whether it was a new storekeeper or a new client! Now you often seem to think that people are not so good, and not so nice, and that they're always talking behind your back.

"And what about the discussions we used to have?" Dovid sighed. "Do you remember, Chanie, how we'd stay up for hours philosophizing about the most obscure topics? And remember how we'd learn together on the long winter Friday nights? *You* were the one who pushed me to review the weekly portion of the Torah with you, and to explain the books on Jewish ethics. You always had some fresh cake prepared for us, and we'd have cake and coffee and stay awake through the hours of learning. Whatever happened to those nights? Now you're always too tired to learn, and it's been a long time since I felt comfortable enough to even suggest that we study together."

Dovid stopped and glanced at me. "Oh, Chanie! I don't mean to hurt you!"

I looked up at him and saw a sight that I had never seen before. Two big tears escaped from Dovid's eyes. My Dovid, my bulwark against the world, was actually crying. He took a handkerchief out of his pocket and brushed it furiously across his face.

"Chanie, please believe me — I never meant for this conversation to take place. Your pain is my pain. I understand it, and I know that it's the pain that's caused you to change. I've tried to be strong enough for the two of us, but I can only go so far." Now his voice broke. "I wake up every morning and I look across at your sleeping face, and as I thank God for restoring my soul, I thank Him for giving you to me, as well. But Chanie, don't you think that in the middle of my prayers I've sometimes started to cry for what we don't have? I too see that space in the corner of our bedroom and remember that we had left it empty so that there would be room for a crib. Sometimes I've had to get back under the covers and stay there until I can force a smile on my face. Only then do I wake you up."

"Dovid —"

"No, let me go on, Chanie. I had hoped that the trip to Israel would help us both. It certainly provided me with the break I needed to reassess my approach to our situation, and for a while I had thought it had done the same for you. When we came back, you had some of that former spark in you and I began to hope that my old Chanie was coming back to me. I held on to that belief for the first couple of weeks, but now everything seems to have gone back to what it was before.

"I'm sorry, Chanie. You cannot even imagine how sorry I am to be hurting you like this. But I'm tired. I'm just too tired to continue to carry both of our loads. I've tried. I really have. Believe me. I didn't want to tell you what I was feeling." He put his head in his hands, and his voice was muffled. "But I have no more strength. I cannot afford to sink into despair along with you. Who would be there to pick up the pieces then? So, it's true. I *have* been escaping. I *have* been going to yeshiva early and I *have* been coming home late. But honestly, Chanie, I've been learning all that time. It wasn't just an excuse. And I did it for us. For both of us."

I was frozen to my chair. "Chanie," Dovid said softly, "think over what I've said. If I'm wrong, correct me when we talk tonight. Forgive me if you can. Maybe I don't even have a right to ask for your forgiveness after what I've said. But I have only you and you have only me. We're as close as only two people in pain can be, Chanie."

With these words, Dovid got up and put on his jacket. As he made his way to the door, he met my eyes and said, "I'll see you tonight."

I nodded wordlessly. The door closed behind him.

The silence in the empty apartment was deafening. I put my head in my hands, and pondered his words. Were they true? Of course they were true. My head began to throb. I stood up to stretch, hoping to relieve the cramp that was starting at the back of my neck. I felt dizzy, stunned. I staggered to the bedroom and stared at the mirror on the opposite wall.

I had stood in front of that mirror so many years before, happily confronting another reality, a reality that had never materialized.

The shaft of sunlight entering through the venetian blinds dissected the mirror into diagonal rows. Motes of dust danced in the rays, distorting the image staring back at me. I walked over to the window, shut the blinds, and turned on the overhead fixture. I was determined to confront my reflection in full light.

The person staring back at me was no stranger, but she did not look as familiar as I had anticipated. She was dressed in a faded housecoat and her kerchief was slightly askew. Her face was still pretty, but it had lost the first bloom of youth. She was heavier than I remembered her.

"Who are you?" I whispered.

The image stared back at me: "I am Chanie." Her expression was hard to read. She looked distant, closed. A little unapproachable.

"Surely not!" I protested. "You don't look like Chanie at all. Why, I'm the one everyone turns to and looks up to, and *you* — you look as if you would feel more comfortable tucked safely under the covers than anywhere else. There must be some mistake."

The Chanie in the mirror stared back at me unsympathetically.

"Well," I told the mirror, "if that's me, then it's not my fault. Life made me a victim of sorrow, of disappointment..."

"Then how would you explain that life has not done to Dovid what it has done to you? He has suffered too but he doesn't look like a helpless victim... He doesn't feel sorry for himself."

"Stop!" I cried. "Haven't I suffered enough? I don't deserve to be called names. I'll show you that I'm *not* a self-pitying victim."

I took a shaky breath, and looked long and hard at that depressed, self-pitying woman in the mirror. I thought of Dovid's tears. Of *his* pain. Of *his* loneliness.

I threw back my shoulders and defiantly met the glance of that reflection in the mirror. "Goodbye!" I said. "I won't be seeing you again. The other Chanie's coming back. The true Chanie."

I stepped into the shower and let the steaming water wash away the years of pain, shame, frustration, and bitterness. I felt cleaner and lighter than I had in years. I put on my prettiest dress and brushed the wig that I saved for special occasions. I dug out the diamond earrings that I had received as a gift on our first anniversary and clipped them on. As a final touch I splashed on some perfume.

I checked the mirror. The person that was reflected there was no stranger, but she was not too familiar either. She looked poised and self-assured and her smile was warm and welcoming. She looked like someone I'd like.

I went into the kitchen and pulled out a gourmet cookbook that I hadn't used in years. I followed the recipe for an elegant yet simple dish and while it was baking in the oven, I set the table with a damask cloth and our holiday dishes. I was arranging the napkins to fan out of the crystal goblets when I heard Dovid's key in the door.

Quickly pulling the phone off the hook with one hand, I tucked in a stray strand of hair with the other. Then I went to welcome my husband as eagerly as a new bride.

CHAPTER TWENTY-ONE

I WOULD LOVE TO TELL YOU that as soon as I made a resolution to change, I found out that I was pregnant. What a nice lesson in cause and effect that would have been! But this book is not a fairy tale. There was no fairy godmother who would wave her magic wand and miraculously produce a child.

I did not become pregnant that month, nor the month after that. A year of months passed and I was still childless. But that year was not a barren one; rather, it was very fruitful.

The morning after my talk with Dovid, I forced myself to do something that I normally would have resisted. I view myself as a creative person, and I usually work spontaneously, following up ideas that excite me at the moment, whether at work, shopping, or cooking. So it took a lot of self-discipline for me to pull out my big yellow pad, take out a ruler and draw a line down the center, and put the headings "Things to Do, Things Not to Do" on the two columns. This was to be the first step in implementing my decision to reconstruct the person I had become over the past few years. Having decided to be totally honest with myself, I realized that not only would I have to break the habits that directly affected who I was, but I would also have to break the mode of functioning that led to those habits.

It took me the whole morning to complete the first draft of this list. I sat at my desk with one foot tucked under me and chewed up the whole top of my pencil before I was able to write down the first thing on my list. In the "Things to Do" column, I wrote, "Call one former friend every week." It took another ten minutes before I was able to write in the "Things Not to Do" column, "Don't refuse the next invitation that comes in the mail." Then things started rolling. By the end of the morning I had listed twenty Do's and twenty-two Don't's.

That was the easy part. Now I had to see if I was really serious about this program. I contemplated the lists and forced myself to choose at least one thing in each column that I would be able to act upon immediately. The first item in the "Things to Do" column would have to wait till evening. It was more likely that my friends would be at home then, and long-distance calls would be cheaper. I also rejected the next five items, for various reasons. Then I studied the seventh one and I was unable to find an excuse to put it off. I got up and followed my injunction to make some phone calls and find out if there were any adult-education classes being given in my neighborhood.

I was pleasantly surprised to discover that there was a wide range of interesting courses being offered. I signed up for an upcoming course in Jewish Law, and one in first-aid and C.P.R. That accomplished, I then perused the "Things Not to Do" column. These things were even harder to implement, since most of the entries involved how to deal with situations as they arose. I finally settled on: "Do not use junk food as a source of comfort," and I went to the refrigerator, took out some fresh fruit and arranged it appealingly on a plate. I munched happily as I reviewed my morning's achievement.

Over the next few months, I reviewed my lists daily, even after I had them memorized. I was afraid to deviate in any way from this rigid strategy, lest I slip back into my old habits. I told Dovid that I was truly involved in "interior" decorating now; overhauling the fabric of my personality could only be accomplished by ripping out and then resewing each and every seam.

Did my Herculean effort work? To a large extent it did. My husband was certainly happier. He looked forward to coming home for a rest in the afternoons and for dinner and relaxation in the evenings. He had never stopped being diligent in his studies, but he admitted to me after the first few weeks of my new program that he was able to concentrate more on his learning than before. He thanked me for making our home a place where he could unwind and recharge. He also acknowledged that I had stopped making him listen to a litany of incidents in which people had hurt me with their tactlessness. Truth to tell, not rehashing these stories made *me* happier too.

My father was thrilled to welcome me back as a full-fledged member of the family. We started visiting each other over the holidays, and he glowed with pleasure over getting his daughter back. Not only had I not given my father a grandchild, but I had deprived him of his only daughter as well.

My husband's family had a bit more trouble adjusting to the changes in me. They had never really understood that I initially drew away from them because I was in pain. Of course they had been hurt when I stopped having very much to do with them, but they are not the kind of people who feel comfortable analyzing relationships too deeply. They had accepted my coldness over the years, probably assuming that I was a bit odd. Now that I started to become involved with them again they were confused, but when I persisted, they took me back and accepted the change in their usual matter-of-fact way.

The hardest relationships to reconstruct were those that I had with my former friends. I just didn't have the courage to call up someone whom I hadn't spoken to in years, and just start to chat. I knew at least that they wouldn't ask me how many kids I had — I was sure that the grapevine had been too active for anyone to make that kind of blunder, but I was afraid I would hear their pity over the wires. I was still not strong enough to deal with that. I kept pushing off the phone calls, but when I received an invitation for our tenth-year class reunion, I forced myself to write back that I would attend.

The evening was a memorable one. I had spent two weeks shopping for just the right dress. It wasn't that clothes were so important to me by that time, but I needed to know that I looked my best if I were to pull off what I hoped for on that night.

I had also purchased new shoes and a new bag to coordinate with the dress. Despite my new finery, however, I had a last minute attack of nerves and I almost did not go. Only the thought that I would have to explain my presence at home to Dovid, kept me from succumbing to my fears.

"Hi, Chanie!" A voice from my past was calling to me.

I turned and saw Leah, the girl who sat behind me in my senior year. "Hi, Leah! How have you been?"

"Fine, *baruch Hashem,*" she replied as we took two seats at a table that was almost full.

I looked around the table, thinking that most of us did not look much older than we had on the day we graduated. My musing was interrupted as someone slid into the last empty seat, which was next to me. "Well, hello, Chanie!"

"Esther! Wow! I haven't seen you in ages. What a treat!"

"When did you all get here? I got stuck in traffic — I hope I haven't missed out on a lot."

I assured her that she hadn't, and that everyone was simply trying to catch up on each other's lives. I hadn't seen my old friend Esther since our painful rift years before. I could see in her eyes that she too remembered the past. "Where are you living now? What are you doing? Are you working?" The questions and answers flew back and forth across the table.

Suddenly the conversation turned to kids. I was waiting. Was I ready? I braced myself. A lively discussion ensued about where everyone was sending their kids to school. My self-preservation instinct told me that it was time to flee and fix my lipstick, but I forced myself to stay seated. Luckily, I had a plate of fruit-stuffed cantaloupe in front of me and I was able to keep busy as the conversation flowed around me.

It was while they were clearing off the fruit course that one of the women at the table turned to Esther and asked, "Do you have any pictures of your kids?" Within seconds everyone at the table was opening their handbags, pulling out their wallets, and passing around their kids' photographs. Everyone but me, that is. I looked down at my plate, hoping to still be able to scrape out some melon rind, but the waitress had just removed it.

"Here goes," I told myself. "The ultimate test."

"Hey!" I said, turning to Esther. "Can I see too?"

She flushed a deep red as she turned to me, stammering, "Um, are you sure you...you really want to see them? They're not such great pictures."

"Of course I want to see them!" I said with a bright smile, while I cried out deep inside me. I stretched out my hand and took the pictures.

"Oh, Esther, your daughter is adorable! She looks just like you. And your little boy is precious!"

"Do you really think so?" she replied, looking a lot more comfortable. "I have a more recent picture with me. Do you want to see it?"

"Sure I do," I answered without hesitation. Before I quite realized what I was doing, I was asking the other mothers to see their pictures too. Soon I was totally involved in the conversation, as my former classmates competed for my attention. I smiled and cooed as I looked at picture after picture, and the stone wall of jealousy that had formed inside me over the years began to dissolve. I was still in pain. Terrible pain! But I wasn't directing that hurt outward. I wasn't blaming anyone — not my friends and not myself — for the children that they had and the ones that I didn't have. I was just grieving deep inside myself, and I knew that I was entitled to that grief.

By the time dessert was served, I was feeling completely at ease with my old friends. We joked around and teased each other with the memories of our school days. I was one of the last to leave, and I left amidst promises that I would keep in touch with most of my class. I must admit that I had a better time that evening than I'd had in years.

The next morning I woke up feeling triumphant. I viewed the reunion as an unqualified success. Now there was only one thing left on the sheet of yellow paper that had not been crossed off. At the bottom of the "To Do" list I had written: "Help parents out with their children in a time of need."

It was not accidental that I had put it at the bottom of the list, even though it was the first thing that had come to mind when I started my lists. It was what the rabbi in Israel had suggested, and at the time I'd felt that my having children was almost contingent upon the execution of his advice. But I had been procrastinating. What I knew I had to do was just too hard. I would be opening myself to terrible pain, and I wasn't sure I could withstand it. Being able to admire photographs of my friends' children was one thing; I had overcome it. But to actually hold their babies and children, take care of them...and to experience what I so desperately yearned for and didn't have... Could I do it? Could I bear it?

I stared at this last item for a long time. Then I turned to a fresh sheet of paper on the same yellow pad. I fooled around for a while until I came up with the following:

This is an ad to be read
  by all expectant mothers:
Are you due soon and don't know
  what to do with your others?
Don't worry about the baby,
  and kids one, two, and three —
When you leave for the hospital
  simply call Chanie!
I'll leave my phone on the hook
  all hours of the night.
So dial 555-3622 in the midst
  of your flight.
No need for you to panic,
  For I'll be there real soon,
And I'll stay with your
  children
From midnight to noon.
By then other arrangements
  will already have been made,
And you'll be no worse off
  for your nocturnal escapade!

Yuck! How I hate cutsie little poems! And this little ditty was worse than most. Did I dare to put it in the yeshiva circular? Did I really want to be awakened in the middle of the night to go and take care of other people's children? Wouldn't I feel uncomfortable going into their houses? Wouldn't they feel uncomfortable calling me? Maybe I should just forget the whole thing.

No! I had come this far and I would never forgive myself if I gave up now. I was sure I could come up with myriad reasons why I should not submit the ad, but there was a prevailing reason for me to go ahead with this plan. That reason was so strong that I quickly typed up the ad, folded it into an envelope, borrowed a stamp from a neighbor, and rushed to drop it in the closest mailbox. Then I sat back to see what would happen.

CHAPTER TWENTY-TWO

IT TOOK TWO WEEKS for the circular to be distributed, and another two weeks till I received the first phone call. When the phone rang in the middle of the night, it took me a moment to remember that there might be a legitimate reason to be awakened at 3:00 A.M. Feeling totally disoriented, I groped for the phone. "Hello?"

"Hello...is this Chanie?" said a nervous, hesitant voice. I assured her that it was. Then she continued and said, "This is Rachel Berg. Remember, I sat next to you at the yeshiva tea last spring? Anyway, I'm on the way to the hospital now. You see, my mother was supposed to be staying with us, but it looks like I'm having the baby a week early, and I didn't make any other arrangements, and I read your ad in the paper, and I thought it might be a good idea to call you, and I was wondering if, well, if you could come over right away? The kids usually start getting up at six o'clock. They have cold cereal for breakfast. It might rain so they'll need to wear their boots to school. They're in the hall closet. The school bus comes at a quarter to eight. The nursery school van comes at nine. The baby drinks soy milk. It's in the top cabinet..."

"Whoa!" I interrupted. "Hold on a minute while I get a

pencil and paper to write everything down. Sorry, but I'm never going to remember all this."

"No, it's okay, don't worry about it. Just ask my seven-year-old for help in the morning. She'll tell you what to do. I'm kind of in a hurry." She stopped and laughed nervously. "Um, when you pull up in front of the house, could you just beep before you park the car? Then we'll know that we can leave. 'Bye, and thanks a million!"

I was left holding a silent receiver. I tried to shake myself fully awake. What was that bit about a seven-year-old telling me what to do? That should prove interesting! And wait a minute! Where in the world did the Bergs live? Should I call her back? I rummaged through my desk for the yeshiva directory and found the address. It was only a mile from my home.

I fumbled my way into the Berg house about fifteen minutes later. The house was quiet and apparently everyone was asleep. That suited me just fine, and I made up my bed on the couch and dozed off until a baby's cry woke me about three hours later. What a sweet sound it was! I got up and washed my hands, barely having enough time to dry them before the bedroom doors opened and a couple of small children came tumbling out.

When they saw me, they stopped short and just stared. I figured that the blonde one in the Strawberry Shortcake nightgown must be the seven-year-old. A little boy with his thumb in his mouth looked to be about four. A duet of crying voices was coming from the direction of the bedrooms, so I knew that there were still two kids who were unaccounted for.

I didn't know where to start. Should I introduce myself to the older kids? Should I go to the younger ones? Before I could even smile bravely and say, "Hi, I'm a friend of your Mommy's," the little boy joined in the chorus of rising wails: "I want my Mommy! Where's Mommy?"

"Who are you?" the seven-year-old asked, yelling to make

herself heard above the din.

Well, at least I knew the answer to that one! "I'm Mrs. Rosenberg. I'm a friend of your Mommy's and Tatty's. They had to go out for a little while and I came over to take care of you. Would you like to be my helper?"

"I don't like you," she said flatly. "I want my Mommy. *Imma!*"

"I want my *Imma.* I want my *Imma.* I want my *Imma.*" The chant bounced back and forth from boy to girl. The crying from the bedrooms grew louder.

"What have I gotten myself into?" I wondered, but then I admonished myself immediately: "Stop it!"

Bending down to the little girl, I said, "Won't you tell me your name? Your mommy told me that she's very proud of you and that you're her big helper. If you would help me too, I'd be very happy."

She appeared to reconsider. "My name is Tova," she said. "He's Avi, and then there's Gitty and Shimmy. Are you a mommy too?"

I gulped. This was going from bad to worse. "No, not yet," I answered. "Do you and Avi want to get dressed and have some breakfast? And could you please tell me what to do with the little ones?"

"How come you're not a mommy? I think you look like a mommy."

"Oh, well, I...Could you just please tell me what to do with the little ones? If you help me, I'll give you a prize," I pleaded.

"What kind of prize? Let me see!" She was now shouting even louder to make herself heard above the cacophony of the rising noise level.

I grabbed my handbag, which was the only thing that I had brought with me. I searched frantically for a pack of gum. Finally, I pulled out a crumpled dollar bill. "How's this?" I asked.

"Do you have one for Avi, too?"

"Yes, I have one for Avi, too. And I'll let you give it to him, but only if you start to help me right now. Is that a deal?"

She nodded, and I couldn't believe how quickly she got everything organized. Having had no younger siblings, I didn't do anything at home until I was in my teens. But this little lady was quite a mover! She took the little ones out of their cribs and had everyone calmed down and dressed, all within twenty minutes! She showed me where all the breakfast utensils were, and where the cereal was kept. They seemed to accept my presence there, and things were running so smoothly that I even ate some breakfast myself.

Suddenly I noticed the time. "Hurry, Tova!" I cried. "Your school bus will be here in two minutes."

I gave her a self-conscious kiss and shooed her out the door. I managed to get Avi out in time also. As he was leaving I noticed that he was wearing one blue sock and one brown one. Well, *c'est la vie*!

With the "big ones" out of the way, I felt less self-conscious. I picked up the baby and began to rock him very gently. I bent my face down to his and kissed him on his smooth and rosy cheek. How good that felt! I kissed his other cheek. He opened his eyes wide and stared at me. Then he smiled. Something inside me came undone. So much sweetness! So much innocence! Did his parents know how lucky they were? I started to sob. I couldn't help it. The tears flowed and flowed and I made no effort to stem the flood.

I sat holding that baby for a long time — I don't know *how* long. It was only when two-and-a-half-year-old Gitty started to want my attention that I was able to reign in my feelings. I looked at my watch and realized that the morning was passing. I washed my face and waited till the redness disappeared from my eyes. Then, taking each child by one hand, I knocked on a neighbor's door and explained the situation to her. She promised to relieve me at noon. The baby took a nap and I spent the rest of the morning straightening up and playing with little Gitty.

I guess I had done fairly well that first time, because it was only a week later that I got my second call. This one came at seven in the morning, so at least I started off the day a bit more rested.

"Chanie? This is Susie Abramson. I don't think you know me. I'm a friend of the Bergs, and I'm due to give birth any day. The problem is, my doctor wants me to come in right now for an examination. I've had a rough night... I really don't think that I'm about to have my baby yet, and I'll probably be home by one o'clock. But it's really too early in the morning to ask any of my friends to come over. They're all busy waking up their kids and getting them off to school. Do you think that you could come over for the morning? I'll wait to leave until I get the big ones off on the bus, so you'll just have to take care of my baby. She's a year-and-a-half, and is usually no trouble."

I told her that I'd be there by eight o'clock. She left for the doctor as soon as I came, and true to her word, I had a very easy morning. Her baby was a placid little girl, and I didn't run into any problems until it was time to change her diaper. The last time I had changed a diaper was when I accepted babysitting jobs about fifteen years earlier! The diapers then were made of cloth, and were secured with big safety pins. Now I was faced with a sopping wet baby and a box of Pampers. I looked around for the pins, but I couldn't find any! Then I noticed the adhesive tabs on the upper corners of the diaper. Aha! I lay the baby on the Pamper and fastened the diaper with the tabs on top. I had either not made the diaper tightly enough, or I had put it on the wrong way, because a short while later the diaper had leaked onto the baby's outfit and onto her crib sheet! I managed to get everything cleaned up (though I was gagging the whole time) right before Susie came home.

I had done what the rabbi said to do. And I had succeeded. Surely I would become pregnant right away. I didn't. What more could I do? What more was expected of me? My lists were totally checked off.

I was bitterly disappointed. For two days I was so depressed that I couldn't get out of bed until lunchtime. But the last few months of working on myself had made their mark: I could not allow myself to remain in a slump for long.

My family-care program gained popularity, and I got called to care for other people's children on the average of twice a month. The routine became easier as I gained more confidence and skills in feeding, dressing, diapering, and disciplining the little ones.

This was a bittersweet time for me. I was in fact doing what I wanted to be doing! I did not feel alienated from my friends. I happily consulted with them on the various aspects of childrearing, and I boasted to them about the cute little antics of my charges. I even bought a car seat so that I wouldn't be tied down if I was watching only one child. Even my car finally blended in with the other cars in the neighborhood, I noted wryly.

But every time I looked down into the face of a little child, a yearning to hold one of my own came over me with such force that I almost could not bear it. I struggled between joy and despair.

During that period I recalled the exact words of the old rabbi in Tzefat: "In the merit of helping others with their children, may God bless you with children of your own" — and I devised a little game that calmed me. When the phone would jerk me awake in the middle of the night, I would silently pray, "God, I am now getting up despite my desire to sleep, in order to take care of someone else's child. May it be Your Will that I will be awakened to take care of my own child." When I had to change a messy diaper, I would intone, "God, I will change this child and clean it as lovingly as if it were my own. May it be Your Will that I will be able to lavish the same care on mine one day."

I would murmur these prayers whenever the intensity of the struggle threatened to overwhelm me. The prayers made me feel closer to God, and their constant repetition granted me the peace that I had never before been able to attain. I took comfort in having chosen the path on which I wished to travel. I had already embarked upon the journey. Now I just waited for God to lead me along its route, as my Guiding Light.

The route remained desolate for another year. I continued keeping appointments with my doctor. I carried on with my work. I proceeded with my social life. But I also felt an inner contentment when I woke up each morning. I was doing everything that I could do. The rest was up to God. Thus I felt unencumbered, and I was able to move more freely. Though there were no markers to count off the miles, I knew that my travels spanned a great distance.

One morning I felt decidedly queasy. The next day I felt no better. I was becoming suspicious, but it wasn't until four days later when I woke up and started vomiting that I let myself acknowledge that I was indeed pregnant. I ran to the phone to call Dovid.

"Hi, Dovid. Listen, I hate to bother you in the middle of learning, but I have a question about Jewish Law to ask you."

"You do?" Dovid laughed. "Okay Chanie — what's your question?"

"Well, it's like this. If we eat something new, like the first fruit of the season, we make a special blessing — a *shehecheyanu*. We thank God for allowing us to have lived to experience that moment. Right? And if we have a special occasion, say, if we have wine at a meal and then get a second, better, wine, we make another special blessing, *ha-tov v'ha-metiv*, thanking God for His bounty. Right?"

Dovid was confused now. "Yes, that's right... So what's your question, Chanie?"

"My question is," I said, "what blessing should I make

when the special occasion has nothing to do with what I eat or drink, but rather with what I *can't* eat or drink? What blessing do I make when nothing that I eat or drink will stay down? Dovid! Do you hear what I'm saying?"

"Chanie, come on! You know I like riddles, but maybe this can wait until I come home for lunch?"

"Dovid, this isn't a riddle! Can't you guess what I'm talking about?"

There was what seemed like a long silence on the other end. "Wait a minute." Dovid's voice was hoarse. "You mean to say that you're...that we're..."

"That's exactly what I mean to say," I laughed.

"Really? Are you sure?" His voice was almost squeaking with hope.

"Sure I'm sure! I'm not a naive little newlywed, you know!"

"I don't know what to say! Oh, yes I do. Chanie — get into bed right now. Please. You shouldn't be on your feet. And don't worry about the laundry or the dishes. I'll take care of everything as soon as I get home. Oh, and one more thing. Drink a glass of milk before you lie down. That's very important. And call the doctor."

"Dovid, Dovid, calm down! I'm not sick. Well, I guess that's technically not true. That is, I *feel* sick! But you know what I mean. This is a perfectly healthy sickness. Don't worry, I won't do anything foolish. But please don't treat me like an invalid. Anyway, I'll let you get back to learning. Your partner must be wondering what happened to you."

On this note, I started my pregnancy jauntily. At least three times a day I stood and consulted the mirror. We had become good friends again. I gazed at the image that stared back at me, the image I had been praying for: my skin was a wreck; I had turned a sickly shade of olive; my cheeks were hollow and gaunt; my body was bloated and clumsy. I was beautiful.

In the middle of my seventh month, I developed toxemia.

The doctor ordered me to stay in bed until I gave birth. But I didn't allow that to get me down. I had made so many friends over the past couple of years that I was never lonely. Someone was always calling to ask me if it would be a convenient time for a visit. I had to buy an appointment book to keep track of all my company! I tried to stagger the visits so that I wouldn't become too tired. All the mothers for whom I'd babysat vied with each other to do me favors. One of them arranged for suppers to be sent in every day. Another kept me supplied with books. A third one kept me entertained with computer games and puzzles. And a fourth one did all of our grocery shopping. Whenever I felt guilty, and feared that I was taking too much of their time, they all assured me that they really enjoyed helping out. They claimed it was no big deal, and it made them feel good to do it. I hope they were telling the truth.

One Tuesday morning I had an unexpected visitor. Someone knocked at the door at about ten o'clock, a time I usually reserved for quiet reading. I asked who it was through the intercom that was hooked up from my room to the front door.

"Miriam," came the reply.

"Come in," I said, not sure which Miriam it was.

In walked a basket towering with things piled three feet high. It was followed by a woman hidden behind the basket. She placed it on the floor next to me, and as she straightened up, I was shocked to see Miriam Fine. I had so shut her memory out of my life that even though I had once known her as well as I knew myself, I had thought that it might be any Miriam but her.

The silence lengthened as neither of us knew what to say. I had stopped being angry with her long ago, but for me she had become a stranger and I didn't know what to say to a stranger. Miriam, on the other hand, was looking very uncomfortable and flustered. She hadn't forgotten me — that was obvious. Her face was suffused with color, and she was looking everywhere but at me.

Miriam finally broke the silence by clearing her throat. "Um," she started off, "I know that you must be quite surprised to see me, Chanie, but I heard that you were confined to bed, and..." she faltered a little "...and I brought you some things that I thought you might enjoy."

I lay there, unable to speak, just staring at her as she began unwrapping the basket. "Here's some rose-scented soap. It's got a very pleasant smell. And here's some peppermint astringent. It will cool you off while you're lying in bed. And here's some cocoa butter to keep your skin from getting rough and dry. I picked all of this up at the cutest little boutique downtown."

She then pulled out a rectangular gold box. "Here's a two-pound chocolate sampler. They've got different kinds of fillings and I thought it might be fun to guess what's inside each piece. The chocolates are from Belgium, and my father-in-law says that they make better chocolates than the Swiss. And talking about the Swiss," she paused to catch her breath, "I remembered that you like cheese and I brought an assortment of that too." She added a few more packages to those that were already accumulating on the floor.

"I stopped by at the bookstore," she rushed on, removing a big, heavy book, "and look what I found — this is a great book on color coordination. The photography is very eye-catching and I thought maybe you could use it in your decorating. I hope you don't have it already."

The basket was only half empty when Miriam abruptly stopped taking it apart. "Chanie," she said softly, still too embarrassed to look at me directly. "This basket was just an excuse to come and visit you. I...I hope you don't mind."

Mind? "Of course I don't mind, Miriam," I managed to croak. "But I am kind of surprised to see you...it's been a long time..."

"I know," she whispered, and then she raised her head

and looked at me directly. "I wouldn't blame you if you asked me to leave, Chanie. But I would really appreciate it if you would hear me out. I have a lot of explaining to do. Would it be okay?"

I nodded. "Let me disconnect the phone, and that way we won't be interrupted. Here, you can sit down on the other bed," I told her as I settled back against the pillows.

"I don't know where to begin," she hesitated. "Maybe I'll start with today. It's easier. See, today was the day that I was finally going to talk to you. I knew that you were house-bound and so I didn't have to check your schedule. I arranged for a babysitter to come at the beginning of the week, and the only morning she had available was Tuesday. I didn't want to call you before I came, because I was afraid you'd tell me you didn't want to see me. Actually, I almost didn't come anyway — I got scared at the last minute, but my husband insisted that I come."

I nodded again, trying to suppress the long-held-down feelings of friendship and affection for Miriam that were beginning to stir, like pinpricks in a limb that had fallen asleep.

"See, it all began with him anyway. When we were going out, I talked about you constantly. Almost everything I said revolved around you! I had gotten so used to following your advice, that I started almost every sentence with 'Chanie says... Chanie does... Chanie thinks...' and so forth. Aaron was constantly interrupting me and asking, 'What do *you* say? What do *you* do? What do *you* think?'" Then, she laughed nervously. "When we got engaged, I was always running off to go shopping with you or going to your house for cooking lessons. When you made us that beautiful *Sheva Berachos*, all I could talk about afterwards was how hard you had worked and how lucky I was to have you as a friend.

"Well, what can I say? Aaron felt very...very threatened by you. Here he was, the man of the house with a new wife, and all she could do was to continue to lean on her old friend. I think he was afraid that you were more important to me than he was. He told me very openly that he would prefer that I have less to do with you. A lot less. I was hurt and upset and I argued with him about it, but I could see that he was terribly bothered by our relationship. This made me confused, too. After all, I wanted to please my new husband. So, I didn't call you..." Miriam's eyes filled with tears suddenly, and she bent down and started rearranging the gifts in the basket. She sniffed the soap and carefully refolded some of the discarded wrapping paper. Only when everything was neatly piled up once again did she continue.

"Then a few weeks after I was married, I found out that I was expecting. You kept on trying to talk to me, but I just didn't know what to do. First I was worried about how my husband would react; and then I began to worry about how you would feel knowing I was pregnant. My circuits were overloaded — I had to close you off. You were always the strong one, Chanie, so I didn't worry about you."

"*Strong* one?" I thought to myself. "You didn't worry about me because you thought I was *strong*? Didn't you understand that my need for your friendship was as great as your need for mine? And didn't you realize that your silence shattered the tenuous hold I had on my ability to cope with my situation?" No, she hadn't realized it.

Suddenly I felt a surge of anger. I wanted her to be aware of the grief she had caused me. True, long ago I had learned how to deal with most of my pain, but deep inside me, in a very secret place, I still harbored a smoldering hurt, and anger at what she had done to me.

I took a deep breath and got ready to speak. I was going to tell her just how insensitive she had been. But as I opened my mouth to begin, my eyes caught sight of Miriam's huddled figure. She was tracing the pattern on the bedspread with her finger, and her face was averted so that she wouldn't have to meet my gaze. She looked so fragile sitting there across from me, that my words evaporated. She too had suffered, and I hadn't known it.

"It wasn't until my first child was old enough to talk back to me that I realized what I had done to you," Miriam went on, smiling ruefully. "I do everything for my kids, and when they answer me back, I feel betrayed. I have to control myself from lashing out at them sometimes and I have to remind myself that they are just kids, after all. I started to think back about what I had done to *you*! You did everything for me too! Why, I remember coming to you with all my problems and keeping you awake until the wee hours of the morning. You never rushed me. You just let me talk, and gently you'd lead me towards my own solutions. You were always so selfless."

I was embarrassed now, and shifted position. "Miriam —"

"No, you *were*, Chanie. Then I went and stabbed you in the back. I pushed you out of my life and pretended that you meant nothing to me. And *I* wasn't a kid at the time. What excuse did I have for my betrayal?"

Miriam did not wait for me to answer, but just rushed on. "I realize now that, had I been open with you, you would have understood. But by the time I realized what I had done, it was too late. How could I call you after five years and apologize? I find it hard enough to apologize for something that has just happened, and when it's for some minor injustice. This was simply too big for me. Aaron and I have sat up countless nights discussing how to right the wrong that we committed. We've prayed constantly that you would have a baby. And we've prayed that God would forgive us, but we knew that we could not merit His forgiveness unless we asked for yours first."

Silence filled the room. It was a good silence. It enveloped us both and a calmness and peace came with it. I felt my baby moving within me. I looked at Miriam and with my eyes I forgave her and thanked her for her prayers. She looked directly back at me and smiled. We were sisters again.

CHAPTER TWENTY-THREE

THE NURSE COMES INTO my hospital room wheeling a lucite bassinet with a pink-wrapped bundle inside. "Are you ready to nurse your baby now, Mrs. Rosenberg?"

It takes me a moment to comprehend her question. Even in my dreams I had never let my imagination travel this far. I had dreamt about being pregnant, about holding a baby in my arms. But nurturing it? I hadn't dared dream so far.

"Why don't I just put the baby in your arms and allow you to become acquainted." She smiles reassuringly. "Then you can try feeding her." She hands me the baby and leaves the room.

I look down at the puckered-up little face, the feathery wisps of dark hair, the clenched fists. I hold her close to me. "You are mine," I whisper. "You are really mine. Precious little soul — God has sent you to me, straight from Heaven. How your grandmother longed for me to have eleven more just like you! At this moment, though, you are enough!" My heart is singing with a joy so resounding that I am afraid its melody will be heard in the corridors of the hospital.

And in the midst of the tune, the joy breaks away, and I shiver. I am in a faraway and desolate place. All I can see is ground so barren that it will yield no blade of grass for decades to come. The wide expanse of land is surrounded by barbed wire. The sky is overcast and the stench of smoke fills the air. No birds twitter and not a leaf rustles. The scene is one of utter destruction and barrenness, and not a cry is heard. All is silent.

But wait! My baby is crying. "Oh, my daughter! Have I already betrayed you, hours after your birth, because I cannot let go of the demons of the past?

"No. I give you my mother's name, little girl. And with her name, I bequeath to you her courage and her fortitude and her undying devotion to God. And may it be God's will that you, in return, merit to repay this legacy with generations and generations of Jewish children who will fulfill her wish to contribute to the nation of God."

I begin to sing gently to my daughter and her whimpering subsides. What do I find myself singing? The words of *Tehillim* that my mother used to sing, the Psalm that everyone had sung in the Displaced Persons' camps:

Zechor davar l'avdecha
al asher yichaltani.
Zos nechamasi b'onyi
ki imras'cha chiyasni.

Remember, Hashem, the promise You
gave me to hope for.
This was my comfort in distress,
for Your words kept on reviving me.

Faiga Nechama nestles contentedly in my arms.

EPILOGUE

THE VERY FACT that God has seen fit to bless many of the survivors' children with expanding families of their own, against all odds of full resurrection, proves that He has not forsaken us. Though our parents have suffered in ways too horrible for us to grasp, it is perhaps time for us to lay their demons to rest.

I recall a conversation I had with my father after the *shivah* for my mother, when we were going through her things. I asked him, "Where are the book and the soap that were always in the dresser drawer?"

"Chanaleh," he replied softly, "that book was the diary your mother kept during her years in the camps, and the soap..." He was silent for a moment, and then he looked at me. "Your mother is buried now and so are they. They will bear testimony to what she has suffered. Let the past be buried, though it will never be forgotten. Now it is time for us to look forward."

God wants us to worship Him in joy and while we can never forget our parents' suffering, and while it must always remain a part of our consciousness and our children's consciousness as well, the time has come to look forward and hope that the future will contain only the love of God for His nation, and not His wrath.